All About Boobs

A User's guide to Breast Cancer and Sex

by

Louise Manson

"Of All the Breast Cancer clinics in all the towns, in all the World. She walks into Mine." ....*The Surgeon*

Front cover: Louise Manson
Surgery & Reconstruction: Professor Iain Brown
Author: Louise Manson
Mermaid photo: Laura Evans www.stives-mermaid.co.uk and Andy
Falconbridge

ISBN 9798477072675

Disclaimer

This is a work of fiction. Unless otherwise indicated, all names,
characters, businesses, places, events and incidents in the book are
either the product of the author's imagination or used in a fictitious
manner. Any resemblance to actual persons, living or dead, or actual
events is purely coincidental.

Dedication:

To James
Delphi & Gabriel

To God and My Surgeon

(they are not the same person)

The Mermaid Centre

The Mermaid Centre, based at the Royal Cornwall Hospital Truro, has provided a gold standard service for more than 20 years. Approximately 17,000 men and women pass through their doors every year. The unit is the largest in the South West, and one of the few in the country offering Oncoplastic surgery.

https://www.royalcornwall.nhs.uk/services/breast/

Acknowledgements

To all those who saved my life and helped me write this book:
Professor Iain Brown, Sarah Zee, Josephine Brand, Imran, Alison
Rose, Michelle Foster, Sara Spary, Pete Green, Andrew Ubogu,
Laura Staeton, Malachy Dunne, Nina Hearne, Caroline Osborne-
Dowle, Tallulah Rotherham, Alex Wedlock, Richard & Amy
Crowther, Kirstin Dennis, Catherine Bassindale, Nick Steele,
Vanessa Roebuck, Kate & Anthony Fagin, Dr Hannah Lloyd-King,
Caroline Petherick, Kerstin Webber, Carla Jose, Dr Andrew Hubball,
David Ingham, Glyn Winchester, Victoria Sayles, Kelly Stevens,
Rose Hilton, Caroline Phillips, Louise & Mike Brett, Lizzy Boyes-
Hunter, Dawn Symons, Annette Arthur, Alison Fox, Karen Slydel,
Sharon Broughton, Jackie Pellow, Julie Simpson, Sarah Alford, and
Leanne Ross Finally... The Mothers: Pauline, Lorelei, Sheila &
Pam.

Louise Manson, mother of twins, author, journalist, university lecturer and survivor of breast cancer offers you: *All About Boobs - A User's guide to Breast Cancer and Sex* which explores the sexier side of the story that no one talks about.

Louise has spent over 25 years working in the media. Cutting her teeth as a health writer for *The Evening Standard*, then writing for most of the nationals including: *The Sunday Times, The Independent, The Express* and a plethora of women's magazines.

It was when she was working at health desk of *The Sun* - commuting by Tube - getting up in the night to feed her baby twins. She decided to relocate to Cornwall and then worked as a freelance writer and did a PGCE whilst living 'the Dream'.

In 2011 Louise was diagnosed with breast cancer. After a double mastectomy, undergoing reconstructive surgery, chemotherapy and radiotherapy she rediscovered a healthy and ever so 'enthusiastic'(ha!) libido and bounced back with her debut novel/self-help hybrid.

Who says you can't feel sexy and have breast cancer at the same time? Louise is the first to break the taboo. Actually, breast cancer and sex are not mutually exclusive and sexiness and surgery can be a thing.

This 'bonkbuster'/bodice ripper?' has sex in every chapter and proves that laughter and phenomenal orgasms, alongside professional treatment can truly enliven your spirit and become an essential (yes, essential) part of the healing journey. She is currently writing her second novel: *Having It All … Please No. You Can Have It Back!*

Preface

If I can't be a good example… let me be a bad one.

The reality of being a working mother of small children … I did everything badly, because I had so much to do, it couldn't be any other way. I couldn't tick every box with a big black tick – it was always a small faded half-tick. My *modus operandi* was if a job was worth doing, it was worth doing badly. I'd written articles about the importance of 'Me time' to avoid mummy burnout. I'd often fantasised about lying in a hospital bed, all responsibility taken from me, being able to sleep eight hours a night. No meals to prepare. No deadlines. No stressed editor on my case. No kids with chicken pox. No elderly parents to worry about. No husband using me as a sounding board for every care and worry. No friends needing air time, on top of that, all the effort and personal care you have to put in to not look half-crazy …No wonder I'd got breast cancer.

1: Charlotte

EVEN when life goes well for a period of time – quite an extended period of time, say a few weeks, months, years – and there is no major drama. There is the nagging doubt that on the horizon some collective negative forces, some dark clouds, are about to descend and wreck everything in the space of 24 hours.

Today was that day.

I could feel the adrenaline and cortisol pumping with extreme precision through every available artery in my body. As I sat waiting in the hospital clinic, my heart was working overtime, my muscles tensed in unison from the tip of my neck to the base of my spine. Like a musical instrument, picking up the rhythm of fear pulsing, at a faster and faster pace, causing a cold sweat to break out in my armpits.

I was learning the difference between the stench of fear and the sweet smell of sweat from exertion in the gym or from rampant sex. I tried to distract myself by reading - yellow and pink leaflets on obesity and alcohol. But I was not obese, and hangovers weren't really an option when you had two small children - who regularly appeared at your bedside in the small hours. I knew the leaflets weren't relevant, but I needed them to try to quell the fear, not that anything could.

I've never worried about my health. Why would I? Or had time for hypochondria. My obsession, I admit, had been elsewhere, namely my weight and Damien in equal measures. If I had to tick boxes about stupid things to do in life, I could probably tick them all. We spend a third of our life asleep – I would spend the other two thirds of that awake thinking about Damien or worrying about my weight. The amount of time I'd spent studying him, I should have been awarded a PhD – and I wasn't even with him. I was married to someone else. Few people get it right in relationships; I wasn't one of them. I had the best and the worst times with Damien. The 'in love' bit of my brain had blown out as a result; no man could repair that. My husband is preferable, though – he doesn't make me cry. I pretty much gave up frequent crying after Damien. Possibly because I wasn't unhappy any more.

I had this secret world of me and Damien in my head, where everything was alright. Just like the early days. Some days I didn't think of him at all; I thought great, I'm over him. Then bang, he was back with a vengeance. I was thinking about him 24/7, I didn't even have a Facebook account. It was like being on a co-dependency diet – having a big cream cake waved in front of your nose and not taking a bite. Such was the addictive process of thinking about him. It was like wild horses – one thought, one trigger, and I was up and running. Looking back the relationship I had with him was always on-off. It followed a familiar pattern: he'd hook me in, I'd become needy of him, and he would withdraw. That was the dance. As for the bathroom scales, I'd never really been fat, but that hadn't stopped the obsession with potentially getting fat.

This was all swirling around in my head now, like a washing machine on its final spin cycle. I sat in a state of misery. What had I done? My attention had been on the wrong things. I should have just been content with Sam and the kids. My experience of life was like being hit over the head by a bigger and bigger frying pan till I got the message. Was this the message?

My GP had said the lump was probably nothing to worry about but she'd refer me just to be safe. It was the word 'probably' that my brain kept short-circuiting back to. How likely was 'probably', or how unlikely was it?

That morning, dropping the kids to school, I couldn't let go of them, hugging and kissing them goodbye in the playground. The teacher had to prise Sophie off me eventually. It was usually the children who were clingy, not me. Normally, I would peel their fleshy fingers off one-by-one from my shoulders. But today, I couldn't explain my notably strange antics to Felix's rather dullard teacher on playground duty, Mrs. Collins, with her raised inquisitive eyebrows. I was usually a 'dump and run' mum; I rarely stayed for the gossip, petty stresses and usual bitching with the other mums who didn't work. But whose obsession with me – maybe because I was a DFL (down from London) – bothered me. Although I secretly envied their coiffed appearance, I was more a throw-on-anything-clean-you-can-find, usually a uniform of black skinny jeans, T-shirt and cargo jacket. But this morning, I knew I was likely to break down in tears if I attempted to reveal to anyone the sheer enormity of what I might be told at the hospital today. Catching a glimpse of Sophie through the window, laughing with her friends, all in similar miniature blue and white checked gingham dresses mesmerised me. Her dark almond-shaped eyes, button nose, cupid mouth and curly blonde hair. I felt waves of agony at the thought of ruining her life, by leaving her motherless. The pain was so intense, I would have done anything just to stop feeling it. Luckily, the agony didn't last, and soon broke away to feelings of guilt, about spending my entire life in such a rush. Not appreciating my family – Sophie and Felix, my husband Sam. 'Slow down – smell the coffee, the roses' all those endless women's features urged. And yet although I had worked on those magazines and with the journalists writing them, I was certainly guilty and more stressed than the weary Trying-to-Have-It-All readers.

After dropping the kids off at school, I didn't have to be at the hospital until 10.30am. I ran like a demon round the lake, a mile or so from my house. The sea was on one side, the man-made lake on the other. I was one of the lucky ones, or so I thought – having moved from London to Cornwall for a better quality of life and air but still managing to garner a reasonable income. That all seemed ironic now – a better quality of life, would I even have a life at all?

I used the trees that circled the water as marking posts to motivate me, rather than the bus shelters of west London, my former stomping ground. I wanted to shake off that feeling of doom before the appointment, but this wasn't humanly possible.

Now, my ankle was in agony as a result. Sitting on a grey moulded plastic chair, I was resting one leg on my opposite knee, whilst massaging my swollen ankle intermittently to ease the throbbing.

I knew secretly that running wasn't good for me. I didn't have a runner's body or mind. But some exercise addict – a friend of a lycra-friend – had said, 'Nothing strips fat off your body like running.' I couldn't get this thought out of my head. But now, I couldn't get the thought of dying, coffins and hearses driving off at great speed out of my head either.

****

'Charlotte James,' the nurse called across the waiting room…of doom. I glanced up and gave her the prerequisite worried smile.

I was shown into the room with the mammogram equipment; it was clinical and windowless. I faced the indignity of scooping up and cramming my 40-something boobs into the metal clamp to be photographed. I focused on the nurse's arms. Her short-sleeved royal blue tunic gave way to huge creamy pink bingo wings, borderline on sides of cooked ham. Probably a calorific accumulation from years of well-meaning patients proffering tins of Quality Street. In the same way, as the well-fed-post-Christmas-supermarket-shoppers dispose of their tins of Quality Street and Roses into the food cages for the homeless. They feel a surge of do-gooding, knowing their bingo wings are safe now the chocolates are away from temptation.

The cold iron scanning equipment was now digging into my collar bone. I had the urge to snuggle up to the nurse for a cuddle, laying my head on her large breasts that were a challenge for the seams of the light blue tunic, and belied any hint of a waist definition, probably for well over a decade. I wanted her to stroke my hair and tell me everything was going to be okay, as I did with my children when they were scared and they needed me to contain their fears. But I didn't get my mummy moment to soothe my anxiety – the nurse had the next anxious patient to attend to and my own mother was dead.

'Press harder, I know it's uncomfortable,' the nurse said. So, I complied.

Finally, I was wrestling to get my t-shirt and bra back on – in a panic and without realising, I'd twisted the straps up at the back, my hands were shaking that much. I couldn't work out why my clearly post-pregnancy 34C boobs were being garrotted by a bra that had fitted when I'd put it on this morning.

'But my children are so young,' I said to the nurse.

'I'm sure you'll be fine,' she reassured me, sounding genuine.

I was now sitting in a side room with a different nurse, not the one who'd said it would be fine. Liar, liar, liar – it was definitely *not* fine. They were not letting me leave the hospital. The results would not be coming by mail in a fortnight's time. The scan had shown up something but they were not really sure what it could be. I was to be subjected to a core biopsy - aka the meat slicer.

It felt as if my left breast was being stapled. A tiny portion of my boob was shaved off, with a little piece of my soul, which was now missing and on a slide in a lab somewhere. It was being peered at by men and women in white coats who'd paid attention in science lessons at school.

Suddenly, my boobs – which I'd always liked, or at least not disliked, as they weren't too big nor too small – had become ticking time bombs. Or had they? A brief review of my boobs would be that I didn't have boobs, or at least nothing to speak of, until I was 30. I'd been a flat-chested teenager. I mentally trawled through the history of my boobs: my first kiss (they are connected) with 'Dan, Dan, the left-wing man,' a 15-year-old rugby player. I was at a party at the tennis club, we were drinking cider behind the clapboard club house - which badly needed a lick of paint. It was a balmy summer's evening I was wearing a puce sundress with ribbons that did up on the shoulders. I could still feel that hot flush of embarrassment when Dan looked down at my non-existent chest – the mutual disappointment hung in the air.

Hitting 30, that all changed; I grew breasts overnight. My friends were convinced I'd had a boob job, which amused me – I would never have one. Suddenly, I had substantial C-cup rounded boobs with protruding raspberry - coloured nipples.

****

Now in the side room, time stood still. I was being offered copious cups of tea to pad out the 45-minute wait. My headache was a mixture of steel-rod tension and caffeine overdose.

'We have a one-stop shop here,' said the po-faced radiographer, as he poked his head round the door, clocking my Botox-rabbit-caught-in-the-headlights look. 'At other clinics, the wait is much longer.'

'It's crazy,' I said to the nurse; she handed me a sludge green plate of custard creams and bourbon biscuits, which I declined for the second time. I felt so nauseous – would I ever feel hungry or eat again? 'Half the female population of this country are having boob jobs and the other half are getting breast cancer,' I said.

The nurse paused, then quietly mentioned, 'Some women say getting breast cancer has had a positive effect on their lives.'

Fuck that – you're not selling me that, I thought - but didn't say it out loud.

Next, I was shown into the examination room and given a chair. Suddenly the door flung open, in strode the consultant: 'I'm Richard Jones, consultant breast surgeon. You *have* got breast cancer,' he said in the most confident voice, with no ifs, buts or maybes about it. He sounded almost pleased – certainly not upset or surprised.

It was the end of the movie, this dark curly-haired brainbox had just announced my imminent death and all I could think was: My god, he's hot.

It must have been the shock – my cognitive skills had gone into primitive meltdown. My best gay friend Alex claimed that when faced with death, your sex drive suddenly soars like you are in the last chance saloon. Even if the situation seems inappropriate at the time. Mills & Boon – not that I'd read one – has got a lot to answer for when it comes to surgeons. Alex went through a particularly sluttish phase in LA, where he worked in the film industry after his sister died in an road traffic accident. It's the basic animal instinct that gets fired up in a life-or-death situation, he maintained. So, I was happy to run with his theory.

'But I'm healthy,' I pleaded with the consultant - like an alcoholic who claims to have had just a couple of drinks when faced with cirrhosis of the liver. 'I went for a run this morning.' I was unable to really take in what he had said.

'It doesn't work like that, I'm afraid.' He smiled, cocking his head to one side as if trying to work out the best way of dealing with me. 'But we can make you better and give you a perfect shape.'

The technical term was 'fall', I was later to discover this. Your fall can be measured – not an idea thought up by a postpartum doctor, I would imagine. Women's golden reward from Mother Nature for breastfeeding is droopy breasts. Strangely, I didn't wish to know my fall score. Numbers on bathroom scales and ATMs had been enough of a torment all my life without adding something new to the mix.

To sum up – I had breast cancer, and I was being offered a boob job.

'You'll probably need a lumpectomy and a bit of radiotherapy,' he continued as if it was a minor inconvenience or the choice of menu in a restaurant. Not some life-changing moment/potential death scenario. 'Will you let me examine you?' asked Mr. Jones.

'Okay,' I said, suddenly wishing he was (a) female or (b) male - but ugly or (c) male – but very, very old – although, if he was very, very old, he might be a bit of a letch.

'Sit on the couch here and take your top off.'

I did as I was told reluctantly for once, feeling embarrassed at first by my still twisted-up bra and then by my semi-nakedness. God, I was going to have to get used to this - whipping my top off for all and sundry - I realised. Topless swimming in the South of France with Damien, in my late twenties, is as far as it had gone even though being topless was *de rigueur* there. Besides, that had been the start of a love affair. Typically, Damien was not content with me just being topless – he would dive under the salty water, and adeptly whip off my neon orange bikini bottoms as well. I would be giggling and laughing, choking on seawater as I tried to stay afloat doggy paddle style, with this horny piranha yanking at my nether regions. We'd exchanged intimate salty kisses whilst trying not to drown. I'd thought in that moment – in Port Grimaud with the sunlight making me squint, the surroundings of the sea, sky and sand, forming a spiritual kaleidoscope – it would last forever, and would always be like that – just me and him. But what followed, was more Brothers Grimm and less of a fairy tale. Looking back, I was so naive, so gullible.

My reverie complete, it was Mr. Jones, not Damien, who was now touching my left breast, with the skill of someone who handles breasts day-in-day-out. But this was not a natural situation for me – it just seemed so unfair that he was so good looking, although he did look goofy when he smiled - Even Kate Moss has to worry about her angles and Victoria Beckham with her smiles.

There was not a lot to smile about in this appointment. I just wanted to jump up and run out of the room, but realised this wasn't an option. If I did that, I would be unable to come back, and possibly die very soon.

It was as if Mr. Jones was kneading bread dough – applying swift confident strokes, to my pale fleshy breast – neither rough nor gentle - just medical. Despite the seriousness of the situation, blushing, I wanted to laugh. Mainly because it tickled, but partly in the way that you have the urge to laugh at a funeral, even when you know you mustn't and everyone would look in horror if you did.

I remained mute, and stared into space. Mr. Jones was touching my left nipple, saying: 'We could keep the nipple and you would still get sensation there.'

I nodded, thinking, wow I'm getting some sensation now, I shouldn't be, because this man isn't my husband and I'm possibly about to die.

'We'll see you in a week's time for the biopsy results.'

The examination was over – the bad news delivered. It was Friday evening and everyone wanted to go home. I wanted to go home. I was standing in the reception area surrounded by medical staff. I was the only lay person in a sea of nurses, consultants, registrars and radiographers.

I didn't want to be the centre of attention – everyone was smiling at me. It was my Cheryl Tweedy moment. Everyone wanted to be my best friend suddenly. But I didn't want this celebrity-like attention. I had to resist the urge to scream 'Bugger off! I don't want any of you. I'm playing the wrong part in this movie.' Yet I knew they were just being kind.

After several abortive attempts at trying to get into similar-looking black cars, I located my own in the hospital overflow car park. On autopilot, I slammed the driver's door and yanked the car mirror in my direction so hard that it snapped off in my hands. I fumbled in the bottom of my bag, pulling out a lipstick - minus its top. I applied it, layer upon layer of pink nude, which I suspected extended beyond the outline of my lips. The contents of my bag were smeared in a tell-tale pink.

There are lipstick lesbians, so there could be Cancer with Attitude. If I had to lose my hair, I'd wear a Lady Gaga wig, not a tea towel. I shuddered, remembering the previous summer and Katy in the playground at school. Katy was Ben's mum from Sophie's class. It was the school fete; stall after stall had been erected on the playground. With challenges like guess the weight of the cake and hook a duck. Katy stood alone, away from the crowd, with the tell-tale headscarf swathing her head. She was such a beauty normally, with her slim figure, blonde hair, blue eyes and permanent smile. Even now she managed to pull off looking attractive - despite being bloated from chemo and bald with a headscarf.

Was everyone too busy or pretending not to see her? I wondered. Cancer makes some people feel uncomfortable – they don't know what to say. It's as if they equate it with leprosy, and any contact will infect – better to ignore and walk the other side of the road to avoid any contamination, social or otherwise. So, observing the scene, I had marched up to Katy and said: 'Have you converted to Islam?' The only other mummy in the school wearing a hijab was Ali's mum, and she was Muslim.

Katy's face broke into the hugest smile of relief, she threw back her head and laughed a big belly laugh. Her laugh was so infectious that I started laughing too, I threw my arms around her – everyone was staring at us now, inching forward to say hello to Katy.

****

Sam was at the front door with the kids; I tried calling him several times in between scans, but each time it had gone to voicemail. This wasn't the kind of message you would leave on an answer machine. The angst on his face took the form of a giant crease, forking to the right of his forehead.

'Why have you parked like that?' he barked. He'd heard my several abortive attempts to reverse the car and eventually had come out to investigate. On the final attempt, I'd given up and parked the car skewwhiff, as if I'd been part of a prolonged car chase, ending up in a big pile-up with the car the wrong way up.

I wanted to scream at him 'I've got fucking breast cancer!' but I couldn't; the children were there too, demanding attention and trying to hug me. I summoned all the strength I could muster, and pulled them tightly to me. They picked up on my distress, and so, they wanted me – their mummy – even more.

'Where are your keys? – I'll park your car,' said Sam.

'Leave the car,' I replied, narrowing my eyes. 'Shall Mummy get you a hungry hippo?' I said to Felix and Sophie.

Their faces lit up. 'Yes,' they said in unison.

'Yes, what?'

'Yes, pleeeeeease.'

We went into the house, 'We need to talk,' I said to Sam - in a tone as if I was going to accuse him of adultery. Sam would never be unfaithful – it wasn't his style. He adored me he just didn't have that streak in him.

'Okay, but I'll sort the car and be back in a minute.'

'Not now.'

I tugged at the kitchen drawer – my bribery and corruption drawer – pulling out the last two hungry hippos from the box, handing them to the children - who ran off in search of CBBC.

We were finally alone in the kitchen together and I broke the news to Sam.

'Why didn't you ring me?'

'I did ring you. I rang you three times.'

'I noticed your missed calls. You should have left a message.'

'How could I leave you a message like that?'

'I should have come with you.'

'Yes, but I didn't think it was anything. I mean why would I get cancer?'

'Mummy, Felix hit me,' a tear-stained Sophie appeared in the kitchen, her arms outstretched for a hug.

I hugged her, then Felix appeared. 'Mummy, Sophie hit me,' his eyes circling down to the floor.

'Come and have a hug too.' I pulled him towards me - Sam put his arms round his little family and we all nestled into his broad shoulders.

The tears finally started tracing down my face.

'What's wrong, Mummy?' asked Sophie.

'I'm tired. I'm really tired. I've been doing too much.'

'I love you Mummy,' said Felix.

'I love you more,' I replied.

'And me?' asked Sophie.

'And you, and Daddy.'

Despite the exhaustion that overwhelmed us – having finally got the kids fed, bathed and into bed – Sam initiated sex. It followed the familiar pattern: he massaged my shoulders for a few minutes, caressing my boobs whilst working his way down my body, eventually slipping his hand in between my legs… fingering me lightly. If that didn't work, his strong tongue-game usually would bring me to the brink of an orgasm finished by a seriously hard fuck - bent over the end of our super king-sized sleigh bed.

But this time, there was a kind of desperation about it. Almost like it may be the last time. The scent of Sam's aftershave and pheromones combined - with his fit brown body - were usually enough to arouse me. Not now; I was a block of wood with no give. I tensed when Sam touched my breasts – the breast. Could he feel the lump?

Yet, I was desperate for sex. I wanted the relief of being able to do something as normal as sex, that my body could still do this - despite the shock. Oh, how I long to switch off my neurotic-doom-filled-head. In a dominating way - Sam pinned me down on the bed and penetrated me hard, coming in an instant. It was uncomfortable. I just couldn't do it. Sam rolled off me and started his rhythmic heavy breathing. He was useless after sex. He just shut down, like I didn't exist anymore. 'Love you,' he whispered and was asleep before my reply.

Lying in bed and staring at the ceiling, I was now frustrated and full of fear, playing back the events of the day.

'Is the tumour like Piccadilly Circus in terms of busyness?' I had asked the surgeon.

'Chiverton Cross at first glance,' he'd replied. Momentarily, I was confused; my reference points were only the familiar London ones from the tube map. In fact, Chiverton Cross roundabout, just outside Truro in Cornwall, is busy by Cornish standards, sleepy by London ones.

I dozed off for a couple of hours but then awoke in a panic, having dreamt I was attending my own funeral. Sophie and Felix crying into Sam's grey reefer coat as I, their mother, was being lowered into the ground.

Sam continued to slumber next to me. It's so much easier for men. Sam ordinarily would be dreaming about his next home-cooked dinner. It was all 'guts and goolies' with Sam – that's what my best friend Natasha had maintained, was all that men required. She claimed that for men, food and sex equalled love.

The next day after Sam had gone to work, I was desperate to call Natasha. Sam had offered to take the day off and spend it with me but I'd persuaded him not to, as he'd need to take Friday off to come with me for the biopsy results. We'd agreed it was important he didn't lose his job over this, whereas my income as a freelance writer was feast or famine at the best of times.

Natasha and I had bonded over the years, with tea, cake and concerns about children, husbands and men we liked. For me it remained in my head as a fantasy and was going to stay there. But for Natasha, dalliances with other men are what kept her going – well, that and the gym. I lived vicariously through Natasha's exploits, giggling with excitement at her racy stories, safe in the knowledge that Sam and I were as good as it gets in the happiness stakes. I was Damien's erstwhile girlfriend after all. I really had no worries with Sam.

10 days prior...

The day before my 42nd birthday – Natasha couldn't make my actual birthday – we were in her stripped pine kitchen with the log burner roaring and crackling away, drinking endless cups of tea whilst her mobile rang or beeped incessantly. When that ceased for any length of time, her landline would start up. Her kitchen often resembled a call centre, but it wasn't work. Tasha was an art therapist.

'What do you put on your skin? It looks so good,' she asked, scrutinising my complexion.

'Sleep,' I replied. With two kids and work, I didn't have much time for all that exfoliating and lathering with cream you're supposed to do by virtue of being female.

'Sleep?' Tasha was a party animal who didn't do sleep. Or rather, she couldn't sleep she was so wired – she was on antidepressants and sleeping pills. It was funny how anyone I thought was sussed and happy as I did when I first met Tasha down here; turned out to be on antidepressants. I wasn't a pill popper, and had always enjoyed good health.

I helped myself to a hunk of the lime and mascarpone birthday cake that Natasha made for me, whilst she took tiny transparent slivers every now and then - so to not get fat. She was a rake, a size 8 to my fleshy size 12, but she still had substantial boobs, despite her scrawny 40-something frame. Natasha would probably consume the same, if not more, calories/cake than me. One-by-one, those slivers added up. But I hated gyms and mirrors; I have always found it impossible to get addicted to exercise, unlike my friend.

As well as a birthday, we had something much bigger to celebrate: Natasha was basking in the knowledge that she didn't have the BRACA gene – the dodgy cancer-carrying one. Women who have the gene, such as Angelina Jolie, sometimes have a double mastectomy as a preventive measure to avoid getting breast cancer in the first place. It was Natasha's scare that had prompted me to check my own breasts. I had cried with joy when Natasha had called to tell me her news – I would hate her to have to go through that. I hadn't mentioned my lump to Natasha after what she'd been through – I'd figured it wouldn't be fair or even worth mentioning. It was Natasha's moment, not mine. I respected that.

During the period of counselling, ahead of the genetic testing, Natasha had taken to wearing extreme plunging necklines – halter-neck tops and sun dresses in rainbow colours – despite the inclement weather. It was as if she had 'limited availability' written across her chest.

I confess, I would stare at Natasha's boobs across the table, imagining the horror of a scalpel, slicing through her flesh. Just the sight of her hospital letter marked - 'Breast surgery'- lying on her granite work surface made me flinch with fear by proxy, I couldn't help myself.

I picked the confidential letter up, just to pass the time during one of Natasha's prolonged absences from the room, courtesy of an animated landline conversation in the hallway - with a member of the opposite sex, judging by the way she was flirting down the phone.

'Mr. Richard Jones's clinic' read the letter. Mr. Richard Jones, I repeated his name: a public - school wanker, no doubt. I flung the letter back down on the work top and stuck the kettle on again. I had interviewed many a public-school consultant for work. I was tired of their arrogance and patronising manner, which was partly why Sophie and Felix were at a state primary school – albeit a good one.

****

Just a few days later, on Friday, I was back in the hospital with Sam. Mr. Jones met us in the examination room. He was looking just as handsome as before, without a hint of arrogance. In fact, judging by his lack of plum, and a hint of London accent, he'd not been near a public school, which made him even more attractive to me.

'I'm Richard Jones, consultant breast surgeon,' he said, shaking firstly my hand, then Sam's.

It was not as though I had forgotten who you are in a week, I thought to myself, and am confused as to who you are. I'd thought about no one else. Mr. Jones had become both my god (not just for his looks) and my executioner. He might as well have had 'love and hate' tattooed on his knuckles – or more appropriately 'life or death'.

'The results have just arrived back from the lab,' announced Mr. Jones.

Thoughts...

Take a friend
Get someone (anyone) to accompany you to the appointment. Pick you up and drop you home.

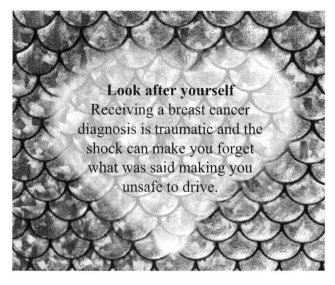

Look after yourself
Receiving a breast cancer diagnosis is traumatic and the shock can make you forget what was said making you unsafe to drive.

2: Mr. Jones

It was Monday morning, and consultant breast surgeon Richard Jones was tired in a world-weary way that belied his 40 years. He sat at his desk, the blinds closed, with his head in his hands out of view of anyone, rotating the thick silver wedding band on his left hand over and over again. Down the corridor to the right was the waiting room - heaving with his harem of needy women. He loved his patients or at least had an attachment to every one of them – young, old, fat or thin – and they loved him. He was a brilliant surgeon, but it was his ability to read women's minds, making each one feel better about herself - that put him at the top of his game.

At work, he felt in steely control – he was admired and respected by his team of doctors, nurses and medical staff. Medicine was his *raison d'être* and had been for quite some time. But it had taken years of hard grind to get to this point, without the benefits of the middle-class upbringing that his fellow students at med school had so enjoyed – their adoring proud families with second homes and skiing trips to Val d'Isère for New Year.

Dick Jones had been the boy from the East End who - despite a series of setbacks - managed to get into the local grammar school in Hackney. But the transition had not been easy for him. Three of the boys from his primary school, who had gone on to the local comprehensive on the sink estate they'd all grown up on, would walk the mile and a half between the two schools once a week and lie in wait for him. They would hide in the back lane behind his school, waiting to beat him up. Ripping his blazer off, pulling at his tie, emptying out his schoolbag – which was usually full of library books – onto the ground, finally grabbing his NHS regulation glasses to accompanying chants of: 'Nerd boy, nerd boy – think you're so clever, but you're just a dick, Dick Jones.'

It was at times like these that his mind would wander back to his early childhood. He really missed his mother – the smell of her Elizabeth Arden perfume and bear hugs at bedtime. He always felt so safe nestling into her arms, knowing that her unconditional love and reassurance made everything better. But it had been short-lived – two days after his ninth birthday, she'd died of breast cancer. He hated birthdays now.

It was losing his mother that had dictated his career path. Dick's compassion and intuition were talents that he had honed from observing his mother and figuring out what she actually needed, usually it was just to talk, which - with an emotionally unavailable husband - was hard for her.

When she got ill, it was Dick's ability, in his innocent childish way, to calm her down and make her feel better about herself in her situation. This would stand him in good stead for his future.

But with the regular beatings after school – which he kept from his dad, as he didn't want to burden him with more heartbreak – he'd not been sure that his dream of becoming a doctor would ever materialise.

To avoid the bullies, he would try a manner of different tactics – hiding out in the hedge till they had got bored and gave up, or leaving by a side door, which meant he could avoid being caught in the back lane behind the science block. But there wasn't a particular pattern to it, they would purposely choose a different day each week, yet they would always find him. After school, he regularly went to the library - which he loved. He felt so at home there. He loved the smell of learning – the embossed academic tomes and the feeling of peace the library gave to him. It took the edge off his grief. He would become engrossed in Encyclopedia Britannica and science books; they allowed him a temporary escape from that visceral pain, that huge hole made by his mother leaving him.

He was prepared to pay the price of the weekly beatings for the magical world of books leading to his quest for knowledge. If he had been willing to forgo his trips to the library, the beatings could have been avoided by legging it straight home from school, making it back before the St Luke thugs got to him. But Dick hated arriving home to an empty house, as his dad - a coach driver - didn't get home till six. The grief of his mother's passing was still fresh - the memory of her perfume still hung in the air, particularly in his parents' bedroom. His dad did the best he could but struggled - as most men did in those days - without female influence around. Bill Jones clearly loved his son, but he lacked the ability to run a home and raise a child. Dinner was invariably bread and cheese, tinned soup or baked beans on toast. It would have been easier for Dick if he'd had a brother or sister, but his mother couldn't have any more after him.

It was while she had been pregnant with Dick that Eileen Jones had found a lump in her breast. She kept it a secret until he was born, intuitively knowing it would not be good news. A week after Dick's arrival, she broke the news to her husband, so they went to the doctor together. She was told at the hospital that she had an aggressive form of cancer that had spread to her lymph nodes. She had immediate surgery, chemotherapy and radiotherapy – juggling a newborn at the same time as treatment – but she did it. Dick's fifth birthday was a double celebration in the Jones household. She got the all clear; they could live happily ever after. Eileen knew having another child would be a blessing, but could compromise her health. Besides, she had more than most people – a lovely husband and adoring son. She was a happy woman indeed. Sadly, this was not to last.

****

Mr. Jones was pulled back into work mode as Jane, his meticulous 60-something secretary, came bustling through the door with the bundle of that day's patients' files. 'How are we today, Mr. Jones?'

'Good, thank you Jane, really good.'

Mr. Jones had spotted his first patient, a retired primary school teacher, in the waiting room earlier. She had one those tell-tale signs, clutching a pile of A4 sheets, presumably hot off WebMD. She'd requested a second opinion after his colleague, Mr. Khan, had diagnosed her. He knew instinctively that a medical dictionary had been swallowed and was about to be regurgitated word-by-word over him for the next hour.

'Hi Mr. Jones,' announced Melissa, his current medical student. She swanned in displaying a five-mile-smile.

'Good morning Melissa,' replied Mr. Jones eyeing her skirt.

Melissa looked downwards, dropping her bag in the middle of the floor, bent down. Her black thong clearly visible from outer space through her tights. She slowly gathered her bag back up – turned towards Mr. Jones - flicked her hair and gave him a cheeky grin. He looked at Melissa with a disapproving stare.

He didn't like Melissa – this was her fourth week with him - he didn't know how he was going to last another month of her standing too close to him, before moving to her next internship. It wasn't that she wouldn't make a good doctor, he just didn't trust her; it was as if she was plotting something. He was sure her skirts were getting shorter as each week went by – yet sadly, her legs weren't getting any thinner nor longer to match the micro hemlines. But he knew that if he mentioned skirt lengths, she would get the wrong idea and report him to the British Medical Association for something he was entirely innocent of.

'Are you ready?' he said to her. She nodded and they headed off down the corridor together – her tugging down at her black miniskirt – to meet his first patient. Just outside the door of the examination room, Mr. Jones stopped for a split second, racking his brain to think of some entertaining line to introduce himself to this potentially-difficult, eighty-something, retired teacher. But his thoughts were interrupted- his mobile in his pocket started to vibrate. It flashed up 'JJ', and as much as he was desperate to speak to Jasmine, his wife – she was the only person he ever really wanted to speak to – he had to kill the call.

Hunched in the corner of the examination room was Dorothy Niels - her paisley hospital gown laying untouched on the examining table. Mr. Jones strode confidently through the door - as was his style - he took one look at the 81-year-old spinster and was immediately transported back to his childhood - his mother reading to him 'Baba Yaga' at bedtime. With her grim expression, hairy mole on a large protruding nose and chin. Dorothy had an uncanny resemblance to the witch from Russian folklore - which was enough to freeze any child – who lived in a hut on the edge of the forest. After his mother had died, Baba Yaga would loom large in his boyish nightmares; as a result he endured the indignity of wetting the bed till he was 13. With all this rattling round in his head like a game of Mouse Trap, he glanced over at Dorothy's tweed suit, fawn jumper, sensible shoes and impenetrable support stockings. 'Hello Mrs Niels, I'm Mr. Jones,' he said, shaking her gnarled twisted hand - dappled with liver spots - whilst trying to regain his composure.

'Mr. Jones, whilst I'm not a medical doctor in the sense that you are, I do have a PhD,' she announced in her home counties accent.

'My apologies, Dr Niels.'

'Apology accepted.'

'I understand you've seen my colleague, Mr. Khan.'

'Yes, I did. He looked about 12.'

'He's 44 and older than me – not by much, admittedly.'

'There's nothing wrong with me.' She barked.

'That's debatable. So, you used to be a primary school teacher?' asked Mr. Jones sporting his widest grin.

'Yes.'

'So, when I tell you what I'm about to tell you, I don't want you to put me over your knee.'

Dorothy's eyes lit up, she started a rheumy cackle of delight, so much so that, for a moment, Mr. Jones got a vague glimpse of what she must have been like as a young girl, long before disappointment and old age set in, giving her karma face.

Mr. Jones waited till she had composed herself again. 'The lump we have found in your breast is malignant. Therefore, will require immediate removal followed by a course of radiotherapy. Did Mr. Khan explain to you what would be involved?'

'Yes, he did. But there are two things to note here: firstly, I grew up in India when it was part of the British Empire, we had a lot of servants. Secondly, I have a very busy schedule – next week I'm on an academic tour, reading from my latest paper on education.'

'You write academic papers – that's impressive.'

'Would you like a copy of my latest paper? It's on the significance of syntax.'

'Why yes. Let's make a deal: I read your paper, and you agree to surgery in two weeks' time.'

'Will *you* be doing it?'

He nodded. 'As it's you, I most certainly will be,' he smiled.

For the rest of the day, Mr. Jones's patients were back-to-back, and it was 5pm before he listened to Jasmine's message. Even at lunchtime, he'd only had the chance to grab a sandwich - filled with what looked like grey paste - from the lunchtime trolley and a coffee from a plastic cup, courtesy of the vending machine. The moment he'd bit into the sandwich, his bleeper went off.

Dick knew it wasn't going to be good news from Jasmine – certainly not what he wanted to hear. He knew he was going to the proverbial empty well with a bucket. Expecting things to be different, but it never was with her.

He finally listened to her message - her high-pitched voice competing against a backdrop of screeching police sirens and traffic noise - all he could make out was, 'I'm in Knightsbridge,' then he heard a huge sigh before the phone cut out.

Dick felt anger tightening its grip around his already tense neck and shoulders coursing down his spine. He had no intention of calling her back now.

He pulled out his leather wallet, checking that his platinum card was still there – which it was – and the wedding snap of him and Jasmine taken some ten years ago fell out onto the floor. He picked it up and traced the creases of the well-worn picture. He had been the happiest man in the world that day, that was apparent from his wide-open smile in the photo. He couldn't believe his luck that he had managed to get such a gilded creature to marry him. Jasmine looked stunning – she still did – her honey-coloured hair catching the last rays of hazy September sunshine, her huge brown almond eyes - which made most men weak at the knees, certainly captured him as well - gazing straight into the lens.

Jasmine had that slim, curvy body that most women obsessed about but found impossible to attain. As for her breasts, by some miracle of nature, they had natural uplift possessed only by his patients after a reconstruction. Motherhood had left no lasting imprint on her svelte frame. Not even a stretch mark. After he had qualified as a surgeon, marrying Jasmine had completed the fairy tale. He would never take her for granted he had been determined to make it to consultant - which he did - before he dared to propose to her.

****

Dick looked at his watch. He really needed to go home, but he wanted something to distract him from his feelings of exasperation, like a toddler needing a toy to stop the wailing; only his wailing was internal. He picked up his Dictaphone, patient notes and pressed Record dictating a GP letter:

Dear Dr Henderson

I met with this old bat today who doesn't know her arse from her elbow and is, possibly the most patronising racist old cow on the planet. I don't actually care whether she lives or dies. I'm just trying to do my job as in: save lives – the ones that want to be saved, that is.

Dick was going to have to speak to Jasmine tonight; there was never going to be a right moment. He couldn't stand it anymore. Apart from when he was at work, he spent every waking moment feeling the disappointment of what she was doing.

He picked up his Dictaphone again, pressed delete and started again:

Dear Dr Henderson

I met with this very intelligent, 81-year-old former primary school teacher who, has been diagnosed with Grade 3 multifocal carcinoma ...

Thoughts...

For Shock

Eat a banana.
They are high in Potassium
and can reduce blood sugar
spikes, unlike chocolate which
causes them.

Sex Shop
@sexwithcancer is a new
online shop which helps
people with cancer take
control of their health.
www.sexwithcancer.com/

3: Natasha

Natasha was at the gym, pounding the treadmill with such determination that, a river of sweat was coursing down her face through her caked-on Belisha foundation which accentuated her lines. She was too vain to get glasses, and didn't realise the landslide on her face. Clad in miniscule cycling shorts and a purple Lycra crop top you would never guess she'd had twins from her tiny frame and fat-to-body ratio, which she kept a close eye on.

She was a regular fixture there such was her addiction to endorphin. She was surrounded by the usual bevy of young men – her boys, or so she thought of them. They were beautifully sculptured muscle-bound Adonis' 20 - somethings not blessed with a brain cell between them, but they were driving her peri-menopausal hormones wild with desire.

Natasha was screeching along to Adele's: *'We could have had it all'* on her headphones – she was so lost in the music that she didn't hear her mobile ringing or Charlotte's name flash up on caller ID nor the text saying: *CODE RED. CALL ME URGENTLY!* – her and Charlotte's shorthand for 'I'm in deep shit, we must speak.' Natasha had been known to text Charlotte: CODE RED if she had gained as much as 3lbs in weight or, usually more so when she had a new love interest.

Natasha was too busy thinking about her ex, Luke. She spent a lot of time thinking about him – too much time. He was the one who got away, or so she thought. Luke was such a contrast to her husband, Mike, whom she'd been married to for 17 years.

Luke was a wealthy, entrepreneurial-businessman. He really did bring home the bacon, but didn't have a clue what a washing machine was or how to work it. He had never grasped the mechanics of childcare in any shape or form. But to Natasha, Luke was the sexy dynamic alpha male that she'd found herself with, after *trop du vin rouge,* in compromising situations at soirées in his four-storey Georgian house.

Mike on the other hand, was slow, dependable; a plodder, who picked up dirty washing from the floor without being asked and was always on tap to do the school run. He ran his own artificial lawn & turfing business from home. He regularly collected money - off vouchers -which he stuck to the fridge door with an oink! oink! pig fridge magnet, much to Natasha's annoyance.

Natasha yearned to be wined and dined by Luke. In five-star London restaurants - the ones trending in Saturday's Guardian - followed by a rampant fuck for dessert. She didn't want to be taken to budget bistros, only to be, staring across the table at a husband she had nothing to say to, and no interest in what he had to say either. And for the evening's grand finale Mike pulling out his wallet and flicking through his scrupulously saved, money-off coupons. Although sex-wise, things appeared good between Natasha and Mike – or so he thought, as they had sex frequently – Natasha could only be moved to orgasm by thinking about Luke. She was heavily reliant on those episodes with Luke to fuel her sexual fantasy.

In their 20s, Natasha and Luke had been an item for five years. They had made an attractive pair – Luke with his dark, swarthy looks and Natasha, the blonde bombshell. Though they had made a pact to play the field for their university years, they would always come back to each other in the holidays. Later, Natasha would reminisce to anyone who would listen, about those long hot summers with Luke on the beach – the sun going down, drinking cold beer and smoking roll-ups. She was on the pill, their sunburnt, sandy bodies rubbed together rhythmically making it, a halcyon time.

After university, Luke had moved to London to work in the City – he wasn't ready to settle down; Cornwall wasn't big enough for him. Natasha, with her degree in art history, had stayed in Cornwall to do her teacher training. She worked at a local college after qualifying, which was how she had met Mike. He was an art technician, who had found reasons to visit Natasha in the art room. He was ready to settle down, and proposed to her within weeks. Natasha, still hurting from what she perceived as rejection by Luke, had agreed - on the private basis that she was pushing 30 and felt her biological clock was counting down.

When they were young, Mike had resembled Luke, but character wise they were opposites. And then, whereas the onset of middle age only seemed to enhance Luke's looks and chiseled jaw, it had the opposite effect on Mike. He wore his disappointment with life on his face, accompanied by a permanent furrowed brow. Whilst Luke got his shirts from Jermyn Street, Mayfair, Mike scoured charity shops for ill-fitting clothes which did nothing for his paunchy figure.

Five years on, the expected babies didn't arrive. Natasha and Mike embarked on IVF on their meagre wages. The doctors could not come up with a reason as to why they couldn't conceive. The seeds of Natasha's resentment towards Mike were being well and truly sown. She knew in her heart that Luke could make her pregnant in one go - up an alleyway or preferably on the cream leather seats of his petroleum-blue Audi TT, with his super alpha male sperm, as opposed to Mike's plodders. Luke always had brand new cars, whilst Tasha resented having to drive the battered and deeply unsexy maroon people carrier that was always about to conk out. But while she fantasised about a trip to London to see Luke, she knew courtesy of the grapevine that he had recently become engaged to Augusta, an English socialite whose father owned half of London including a plethora of Grade II listed garden squares sporting the family crest.

With nothing to lose except large sums of money, Natasha and Mike had plunged all their savings into a further two rounds of IVF. When that failed, they had re-mortgaged their modest terrace house. After the fifth IVF attempt, they had been presented with twin boys, Charlie and Samson, who were now 10.

Natasha found them a real handful; he couldn't see that it was her lack of discipline that was making them so. On hearing she was expecting twins, Natasha had confided in Charlotte, that she was desperate for girls, then boy/girl – twin boys was definitely her third choice. It was an unspoken tension between her and Charlotte, not only was Charlotte happily married, but that she had the perfect family – a girl and a boy. If ever seven-year-old Sophie entered the room, Natasha would gaze at her adoringly and reach out to cuddle her, saying things like, 'What a pretty dress you have' or 'You're so cute.' But now at 45, it was unlikely that Natasha would get the daughter she so wanted.

Several years later, Luke having made his money moved back to Cornwall, purchased the biggest house he could for Augusta and their four children – two girls and two boys – and lived in domestic bliss. He was a contented man.

'Luke only has to brush past me and I fall,' Augusta had confessed to Natasha the first time they met. 'He's had the snip now,' she'd giggled. From early on, Augusta had no suspicions about Natasha and Luke. She was aware of her good fortune in life, always saying to Natasha *mi casa es su casa*, always inviting her over for wine suppers and festive parties, even though Luke wasn't so keen. Augusta was the perfect host she and Luke had become renowned for their exquisitely catered parties with waiters handing round canapés on silver trays. They weren't the sort of parties that Natasha and Mike were accustomed to in Cornwall, where you were expected to bring a bottle of plonk and a quiche that you'd made.

It was Luke and Augusta's second Christmas in Cornwall when Luke and Natasha had their first lingering kiss after a gap spanning two decades. There had been a lot of sexual tension between them leading up to that point, but it still came as a surprise to both of them – well, to Luke at least.

Luke's house was twinkling with white fairy lights. Wreaths of holly and bright red berries were festooned around the walls, mistletoe hung from chandeliers. Natasha – who squeezed herself into a figure-hugging flaming red Bardot-style tube dress – was being regularly topped up with champagne by a spotty young man in a stripey uniform who knew exactly what he was doing, he didn't care if he got the sack. The risk was worth it, for this up-for-anything 40-something woman. It wasn't him Natasha had her eye on – it was Luke – but any male attention was good.

She had to find a way of distracting Luke from Augusta, who looked simply stunning in a Nigella-like off-the-shoulder LBD. Augusta was voluptuous, all hourglass figure and big boobs, she glowed with happiness – her life couldn't be better. She loved Luke, and her four children were healthy. She was a lucky woman. She and her family wanted for nothing.

Sometime earlier, Luke and Natasha had run into each other in town, he had mentioned to her that he'd found some old photos of them as teenagers. Natasha was more than keen to see them. This would be her opportunity and with that thought, she downed another glass of champagne and went off in search of Luke.

She was up and down three floors in her Jimmy Choo kitten heels, that she had bought used but in good condition off eBay. They were killing her in spite of the copious amounts of champagne she'd quaffed. But no pain no gain, she figured as she hoiked up her dress and clambered up yet another staircase in search of her prey. At last, she found him on the roof terrace alone, having a cigarette, the light from the outside heaters lighting up his face in full, as he looked out to sea.

'Could I have a drag on your cigarette?' asked Natasha.

He turned and looked her up and down. 'I thought you'd given up?'

'I have – don't tell Mike, anything goes when I've had a drink.'

He handed her his cigarette. She inhaled and handed it back to him.

'I don't want that now. You keep it,' he said as he surveyed the cigarette, covered in red lipstick.

She laughed and took a second drag. 'Those photos Luke, you promised me.'

'Ah, yes those shots of you in a virtually non-existent pink bikini on the beach. How could I forget them?'

Natasha dropped the cigarette and put it out with her heel, she moved closer to Luke so that they could feel each other's breath against their faces.

He put his hand on her bum for a few seconds and then moved it away. 'You've still got a great body,'

'Thank you,' she replied.

'The thing is, Tash,' he paused, 'I'm happily married.'

'Are you giving me the brush-off?'

'I take it things are no better with you and Mike? Is that what all this is about? Look, I'd like to kiss you and touch you – don't think I've forgotten how it used to be.'

'It could be like that again.'

'No, it couldn't. I have responsibilities now. I love my family – they're my world. I won't do anything to jeopardise things with Augusta and the kids. Just because you're unhappy in your marriage doesn't mean you can butt into mine.'

Natasha launched her lips to his. 'Oh, Tasha,' he groaned, he kissed her back passionately, she guided his hand back onto her bum and then moved her hand to his ever-growing erection, simultaneously unzipping his trousers with her other hand, gradually moving him towards the darkness of the roof top.

****

Now, the gym was starting to empty out. Natasha grabbed her water bottle and took a big swig out of it as she wiped sweat from her brow with her towel. It would be the bike next, she clambered off the treadmill and noticed her mobile was flashing. She was hoping it was Luke, but knew it wouldn't be. Not texting him was like starvation, she would have to resist the bite. She knew, chasing after him was not going to work.

She plugged in her headphones as she straddled the exercise bike, she started pedalling as if her life depended on it. 'Lottie, it's me. I'm at the gym,' she gasped. 'I have to whisper, but there's this gorgeous guy on the free weights – he's new here. He must be about 22, those biceps.'

'Natasha – I've got some bad news.'

'What news?' the signal was breaking up and she was only getting every other word.

'I've got breast cancer.'

'You've got what?'

'Breast cancer. I'm in the hospital now.'

Natasha dropped the phone, then, jerking forward to catch it, she misplaced her foot on the pedal. There was a loud crash – the man on the free weights turned around – only to see her fall to the floor, hitting her head as she went down.

Thoughts...

Surgeons

It's important you are happy
with your surgeon. You need
someone who gets you, puts
you at ease and suits your
personality.

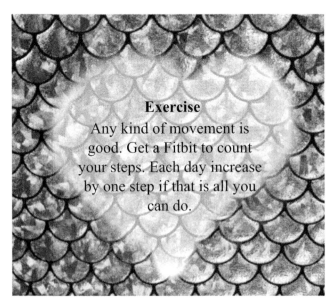

Exercise

Any kind of movement is
good. Get a Fitbit to count
your steps. Each day increase
by one step if that is all you
can do.

4: Charlotte

I should have realised it wouldn't be good news from the two-hour delay in the waiting room, Sam accompanied me. I gazed at the supposedly *feng shui* fish tank – I've never been entirely convinced that the ancient art of Chinese placement, really works for Western buildings. When Natasha's marriage had entered a rocky patch, largely because she was having affairs - she had been told by a feng shui expert that her toilet was in her 'relationship corner'. But she was adamant that she wasn't moving her bog. Things with her husband had been down the drain ever since.

The fish tank was not having a calming and abundant effect on me. I wanted to scream. The wait, unbeknown to me, wasn't designed to torture, it was because Mr. Jones liked to spend as much time with his patients as they needed - especially the ones receiving the bad news - so he didn't worry about the queue in the waiting room. If a patient he was seeing needed a bit longer to digest the results, or ask questions, he didn't rush them out.

The waiting room was now deserted - apart from Sam and myself. We sat hunched without exchanging a word - which was rare for us. We weren't like some married couples who no longer had anything to say and whose very presence irritates the other. Our silence was only punctuated by offers of tea or coffee every half-hour, by the overly-cheery tea lady who knew it was going to be bad news. She had seen it all before, the anxious wait of the last person to be seen.

I had awoken at 4am - even more tired than when I'd gone to bed. I was bathed in sweat, with my leg muscles locked in a tetany-like grip which took a few seconds to wear off. It was accompanied by a dreadful depression which screamed the words CANCER, CANCER, CANCER, with graphic visuals of Dickensian gravestones inscribed with 'Charlotte James, mother, wife, daughter' running round my brain on a loop the minute I would open my eyes. I'd reached down under my oversized white T-shirt and felt my left breast. It must have been the hundredth time I'd done this in the previous couple of weeks. I had poked and prodded the little mass – rolled it between my index finger and thumb. It nestled below my nipple, the size of a Malteser. It was not the garden pea that countless women with breast cancer I previously interviewed as a journalist described it but a honeycomb confectionery ball covered in chocolate - 10 calories if you were counting.

In the bathroom, I looked at my now pale, blotchy face in the mirror – my thick messy dark hair and blue eyes - with increasing dark corners and a mouth turning down at the ends. Looking back at my reflection, I realised my smile had been erased, my happiness snatched away, just in the space of one week. I replayed in my mind Mr. Jones striding through the door and saying to him: 'But I'm healthy – I have blueberries on my muesli.'

Cancer seemed such an alien concept to me – it was not on my radar. It was nothing I could relate to. They might as well have said sclerosis of the liver though I'd never been a big drinker or even had the hangovers my girlfriends experienced. Or lung cancer though I'd never smoked. It felt like getting tennis elbow when you've never hit a ball.

In the hospital waiting room - such anxiety - I could hear nothing but my own heart thundering against my chest wall, palpitations and tightness as I breathed. Never mind breast cancer, I thought, a cardiac arrest was imminent. Out of the corner of my eye, I spotted a flushed Mr. Jones striding down the corridor – he, and a staunch-looking nurse, marched into a side room as if they meant business. Either they were having sex, or something was majorly wrong. Could it be connected with me? Not the sex…I mean. 'It's not always about you.' my late mother would say when I frequently lapsed into self-obsession. If only she were here now.

'I want my mum.' I repeated this silently over and over, like a mantra to summon up her spirit.

Sam, sensing my distress, took my hand and held it in his big man's hand, covering my slender fingers. We sat in silence, until the nurse of death carrying my notes appeared: 'Charlotte James.' she announced.

'I feel like I'm going to pass out,' I said to Sam. I was shallow breathing. There was no oxygen getting to my brain or my legs. 'I'm scared they're going to tell me I will die.'

'I'll hold you up,' said Sam, as he grabbed the scruff of my neck as if I was a frightened kitten.

Stopping me from collapsing on the floor.

The nurse opened the door, we entered the soulless grey examination room. Minutes later, Mr. Jones walked in, Sam and I were both sitting rigid. Mr. Jones was wearing dark-framed glasses which made him look even brainier than he was - if that was possible.

'Unfortunately, we've found another tumour,' said Mr. Jones, 'This *will* change things.'

'How do you mean?' I asked, looking directly at him.

'You will now require a complete removal of the breast tissue on that side, for safety.'

I looked at the floor, too terrified to look up. Scared that I was going to break down.

Mr. Jones continued: 'We can also uplift the other side, and make you even. We can either use silicone implants or your own body fat.'

I remained silent Sam became animated in Richard Madeley style: 'She's got fat all over her body.'

I started laughing, as did the surgeon. The mood in the room lightened – even the nurse was laughing.

'Thanks for that, and your contribution' I said.

'Could you take fat from my stomach?' I was desperately trying to find the upside. There must be one, maybe in the form of a tummy tuck perhaps? - After two children, my stomach although presentable enough in the right kind of understated Calvin Klein bikini, was no longer the washboard it had once been.

'Let's see your stomach,' commanded Mr. Jones.

I unzipped my size 12 - now loose - black skinny jeans, the top of my lacy pink knickers in evidence. I flushed with embarrassment. This morning, I hadn't been expecting anyone to see them, with no recall of putting them on, or any knickers for that fact.

'No,' said Mr. Jones, shaking his head.

What do you mean 'no'? I thought.

'You're too slim.'

'Too slim?' I was aghast. I'd spent my entire life thinking I was too fat. Now that I could put my *avoir du pois* to some good use, aesthetic use, I was too slim.

'I can put on weight!' I said in semi-desperation.

'Are you going to start mainlining Cornish pasties?'

I was silent. Mr. Jones was from 'up country' as they call anyone here who's not from Cornwall, I've observed. The Cornish don't say Cornish pasties – just pasties. Mr. Jones, like me, was also Down from London. The slight London twang in his accent gave him away, but also gave him street cred with brains - quite an intoxicating mix.

While most DFLs are well received in Cornwall, there was a degree of 'you come down here with your London money and your London ways' as most locals grumble "bleddy emmets". There was some resentment over DFLs here – selling up in London for a better quality of life in Cornwall – buying property or even second homes down here, forcing prices up and leaving local people unable to get onto the property ladder, as a result having to leave their home county.

The pasty thing, I was told, was supposed to wear off after three years, and the craving would go. But we still had one every Saturday for lunch, after the children had been swimming, they were famished and needed warming up.

I reflected that on balance my life had been dreamy since arriving in Cornwall five years earlier: two beautiful kids, lovely husband and house to die for. 'You actually did it!' was the most frequent thing my London friends and acquaintances said to me. Followed by: 'Most people just *talk* about moving to Cornwall.'

****

I recalled the moment when I knew I had to quit London and leave it all behind. I had been working as a feature writer for a national newspaper. It was nudging towards midday on a grey Tuesday afternoon in February – I'd just come out of an editorial meeting, on the seventh floor of a tower block in Wapping - with the assistant editor. Although I had several great stories to research and write up they had all been approved by an impossible features editor. I was furious about a discovery I'd made that morning - I was so angry that a part of my brain was about to start a blow-out. The fury was so intense, I couldn't ignore it. It started pounding at my temples and then coursed round my head in a red-hot circuit.

Returning to my desk, I surveyed the sea of paperwork covering every inch of it and the mass of yellow post-it notes stuck to my PC. I pulled them off, one by one to reveal the flashing message on my monitor: 'Your mailbox is full … your mailbox is full.' A large latte that I had ordered earlier appeared at my elbow courtesy of Zac the runner - possibly the next editor-in-training. I went to grab it, but knocked it all over my paperwork.

A combination of sleep deprivation and PMT weren't really helping my cause. I screwed up all the now-sodden paperwork into a big ball, stuffing it - along with the polystyrene coffee cup - into the bin. Grabbing my mobile, pen and spiral notepad I shot out of the newsroom, leaving a trail of bemused faces behind me.

I personally loathe any form of injustice. I was fuelled by a desperate bid to get out of the building and the situation I was in. Determined to escape from the windowless office which stretched the entire length and breadth of the building, I ran up the stairwell, catching my breath in the fresh air as I stood on the roof terrace gazing down at the panoramic view of London laid out below.

The term 'roof terrace' usually conjures up images of champagne-supping, well-heeled types circulating in between verdant manicured pot plants, backed by an inspiring sunset. But this depressing roof terrace resembled the final days before the inhabitants surrendered in some long-term war-torn country. Not surprisingly, few ventured out there, even those employees desperate for a fag break had moved on. So, I was alone.

Tower Bridge was to the left of my postcard view of the city. I thought of all the jumpers that had gone to their death, having scaled those blue and white railings. I craved their oblivion. It wasn't that I wanted to die, I just wanted to not exist for a while - to exit the vortex for a bit. It wasn't about something as final as death- I just wanted sleep.

My phone vibrated in my bag – it was Caroline from HR. I'd already noticed two missed calls from her on my commute to the tube that morning.

I killed the call. What was I supposed to say? 'Hi Caroline. I'm just contemplating jumping from the News Co. building – obviously not a viable option, given that I have two very small children and the amount of paperwork you've already produced on my behalf, in obtaining me a new watertight work contract.'

The lack of sleep I was experiencing was borderline torture – the sort of suffering experienced by POWs purposely kept awake with haranguing and lashings. Sophie at 18 months and Felix at a bit over two years had been born less than a year apart. I had assumed I'd only be able to have one child, as Felix had been four years in the making – yet it had taken five minutes to start to produce Sophie. I think it must have been an immaculate conception or necrophilia, I was so dead tired at the time I didn't recall any action in the bedroom. After she was born, the babies took it in turn to wake up at night. On a bad night it could be every hour. From day one, Sophie was never going to be a good sleeper. I had tried everything, including Gina Ford's *Contented Little Baby* book. My health visitor had told me: 'Don't bother with that book, you won't like it – you're not a rules girl.'

How right she was. One morning after a particularly sleepless night, I whipped open the upstairs window of my Victorian terrace house and flung the paperback at the recycling bin below. It missed landing with a thud on the pavement. Then I had to run downstairs in my pyjamas to retrieve *said book* and put it in the bin. I thought I'd been unobserved, but Guy, city slicker and the local alpha, who always got up crazily early for the markets – financial, not fruit & veg – caught me in the act.

'Charlotte – you're not looking for dregs this time of the morning?'

I glanced down at the wine bottles – two red and two white from Saturday's last impromptu dinner – and just laughed.

'And your pyjamas are… see-through from where I'm standing. You do look lovely though… even at this hour.' And off he went to work in his bespoke pinstriped suit.

The problem was, that on the rare occasion when both the babies slept for the same number of hours, I would lie awake, worried that Sophie had stopped breathing or that my editor would not like my copy – or worse, I would not get the interview and would have no copy at all.

I felt my nerves on edge the whole time, my stomach churned with free-floating anxiety - even when there was nothing to be anxious about.

Going back to work had not been a difficult decision. As much as I loved my babies, I craved using my brain, participating in anything that wasn't baby-related, or having conversations that weren't about nappies. Even loading the dishwasher was a welcome break in the routine of endless changing and feeding. Other mothers I had met seemed to love talking about brands of nappies, feeding and types of buggies. Owning a double-buggy myself meant I was more of a target for baby-bores. I tried to avoid eye contact with other pram-pushers – looking down at the pavement, pretending to be lost in post-natal-depression-land. I also resented all the gear you had to take with you on-said-buggy, and refused to. Other mums loaded their buggies up like a tank preparing to go into battle. I just took my mobile and keys and would cadge a nappy off someone, like a smoker trying to give up - you simply nab a cigarette rather than buy a packet.

But the price I'd had to pay for going back to work was high. I obsessed about sleep all day – totting up hours of broken sleep every morning, trying to forge them into a whole. My whole skeleton ached so much from the tiredness that I wouldn't have got out of bed if it hadn't been for the ravenous skull-penetrating scream of my newborn, that no one unless they were on heroin - could ignore. On a good night I would clock up five hours- but not consecutively. I fantasised about five hours of sleep at a stretch, but I was long off that.

The morning routine consisted of dropping the infants to nursery by 8am, by which time I'd been up for three hours. Finding something clean, not creased and presentable for me to wear was a major challenge when trying to dress two small children. After heaving the two small bundles into their car seats, I was then stuck in gridlocked traffic.

The nursery was on a busy road and trying to find a parking space was difficult. The alternative was walking with the double buggy, which took longer, and crossing the busy Fulham Road was dicey. It would invariably be lashing down with rain or just freezing cold. Felix had a pathological hatred of the rain cover, screaming the place down whenever he got a glimpse of it. So, what with the impossibility of attaching it to the buggy, with all those irritating poppers, the car seemed the softer option. But then when I drove back to the house to walk to the tube, my parking space had inevitably been taken by a commuter.

At 6pm, Sarah from *Baby Park* picked up the children from nursery, taking them to her Ofsted approved house and fed them supper - I would then collect them at 8pm.

For the privilege of all this stress, my childcare bill was nudging £1800 a month. I also worked out that due to the long hours I worked, my cleaner Rita was on a better hourly rate than I was. Rita's main talents were putting her feet up when pissed, shouting at the cat and making my clothes smell of cigarettes.

She would take the ironing home to her flat – a fume-filled box that stank of Benson & Hedges – as she was too lazy to do the ironing *in situ.* I should have sacked her, but I liked her. I loved her Irish accent – she was from Limerick – and her fantastic humour. Besides, her husband, who had been a drinker, had died of lung cancer.

Whilst I found the working week stressful, weekends didn't offer much relief. I spent Sundays visiting my mother in a nursing home, whilst Sam took the kids to the park. My mother had had a stroke and could remember very little. My elderly dad also needed support, in the form of cups of tea, laughs and chats. As he was bearing the brunt of Mum's condition, he regularly needed to share his guilt about putting his wife into care. It was the right decision, but really, he needed reassurance from me - his only child.

There was a constant worry at the back of my mind that I was doing everything badly – that I wasn't a good enough mother, wife, daughter or employee. I was trying to keep all the plates spinning in the air- because it was all about to come crashing down around me. Or at least I'd be found out for the fraud I was. I felt I was breastfeeding everyone - not just my children – Sam, my dad, my employer, my friends, oh, and acquaintances – yet, there wasn't any sustenance left for me.

I hadn't planned any of this – for Sam to be working away regularly during the week, me working full-time, my mother to get sick – I'd only gone back to work part-time. But then I was offered full-time only. It was my dream job, but it was a question of right job - wrong time.

Every day, I would arrive in the news room at 10am. Guilt-ridden, as all my colleagues were already at their desks, pouring over the morning editions, with clothes that matched and make-up expertly applied – my childless-female-colleagues at any rate. But then they hadn't done what felt like the equivalent of ten rounds with Mike Tyson before arriving at work. I would employ a fantasy sequence to get through the 10 o'clock walk of shame past the sea of faces and monitors, with my head held high. There was no way I could get to the office any earlier with my tight schedule, then crossing London on the erratic Piccadilly and District lines.

So rather than anticipating my work colleagues thinking: Late! Late! Late! I would fantasise about walking into the newsroom with all heads turned in my direction. But instead of frowns of disapproval they would all be smiling at me and singing with their arms outstretched *'Baby I love Your Way'* by Bob Marley, then I would join in and finally arrive at my desk all smiles. This technique - which I practised daily - I'd gleaned from a psychotherapist I had once interviewed about post-traumatic stress disorder. It seemed to work. At least it started my day off well enough, although it was usually all downhill after that.

It was impossible to get any copy written in the noisy newsroom with the phone ringing incessantly, editorial meetings, hundreds of emails to reply to and post arriving throughout the day. There were upsides though – a steady stream of freebies. There were things like boxes of Krispy Kreme doughnuts when they first launched at Harrods – a welcome sugar fix in a sea of stressful deadlines – or £200 worth of Clarins biked over to me to pamper myself with - in exchange for a mention of their new skin cream in a feature.

The work style that I'd perfected over the years was to faff around all day giving the impression that I was doing nothing, and then write a brilliant piece of copy at 6pm when the phones had eased off and my research had been done, or at least my thinking time was over. Others, I noticed, spent all day writing one-dimensional formulaic copy but they didn't last long.

When I'd first started at the paper, I'd got what I thought was my first fan letter and eagerly opened it. It was from an 80-year-old grandmother saying: 'Your article was utter tosh.' I had done a piece on 'Breast is Best', extolling the virtues of breastfeeding. She said: 'I didn't breastfeed any of my children, and they all turned out all right.'

****

It was starting to spit with rain, making the roof terrace look even more depressing. I didn't really intend to jump and I couldn't go AWOL either. The impossibility of my situation - like the imminent dark rain clouds above my head - weighed heavily on my solar plexus. I knew if I attempted to flee, I would be wrestled to the floor for the contents of my reporter's pad. I had just got the biggest scoop ever. None of the other nationals had managed to get the story and it would probably run to a double page spread.

My phone sprang to life. It was Max Howard, the assistant editor, booming in my ear with his 30-a day smokers' drawl. There was a permanent waft of smoke around him. If he got too close to me, or whispered something -usually filthy- in my ear, as he'd done a few days earlier, I would start coughing from his Marlboro residue.

'Where the hell are you Lotto? We're going to press on this one.'

'I'm on my way. I just felt ill and needed some air.'

'Make sure you're in front of my desk in five minutes.'

'Sure thing,' I replied.

On the horizon as I looked to my left there was a giant life-sized poster of Jack Rashleigh beaming his one hundred-megawatt smile promoting the new series of the JR Show. Drifting off in thought, I wished I had his confidence.

Max was the last person I wanted to see, he and his sidekick Rachel Wiseman - the features editor, were the objects of my distress. It was widely known in the newsroom that despite both of them being married – Rachel, 10 years his junior, married for only a year, were having - to use tabloid-speak - 'a torrid affair'.

I didn't have a problem with this *per se*, besides, it was none of my business if they were bedfellows. Sleeping my way to the top of the glass ceiling wasn't my thing, but I didn't condemn anyone else for doing it, if that's what they wanted to do in the name of ambition. I preferred success to happen naturally, if it was meant to be. I craved to be recognised for my merit, rather than by stabbing someone in the back or selling my granny for a story. If someone I'd interviewed rang me the next day and asked me to take something out of my copy, I would take it out. Stitch-ups weren't really my style.

I'd written a cracking good story, which was an exclusive and destined for that morning's front cover. A by-line on the front cover would be very prestigious, bearing in mind the newspaper had the biggest circulation in the world. The headline screamed *No More Daddies.* The story had been sparked by a jobsworth at a hospital in Leeds, whom for 'Health & Safety' reasons and reasons best known to himself, had decided to unplug a freezer cable. Unfortunately, the freezer had been stacked not with frozen peas and fish fingers but frozen sperm samples from men who had testicular cancer and had given the samples before undergoing chemotherapy - so they wouldn't miss out on becoming a father at a later date.

That morning's edition had run my story on the front cover. I'd bought a copy from the kiosk before I shot through the tube barrier. Cramming myself into a carriage, one hand on a strap and the other holding the newspaper, I glanced excitedly at the front page; the sub-editor had even run with my headline.

'Fantastic!' I said out loud to the carriage with a big grin across my face. Then to my horror, I noticed two little words blinking at me in the middle of my copy: the by-line 'Rachel Wiseman'.

Two hours later, I found myself sat in the editorial meeting rooted to my chair in shock whilst Max complimented his lover Rachel on her exclusive story and great headline.

I knew full well that to say anything would only make things worse, affecting my position on the paper. Rachel did look a bit sheepish, every time I tried to make eye contact with her, she neatly avoided my gaze.

I'd put up with Rachel's duplicity before - along with her constant nit-picking. Whenever I turned in a great piece of copy, she would make it her mission to find something wrong with it. She'd condemned me over the *No More Daddies* piece for leaving a couple of carriage returns in my copy, on the basis that it wasn't fair to the subs to have to take them out, even though I was under immense pressure going to press for the next day.

****

But now, I'd managed to leave behind all that crazy media world and relocate to Cornwall, life was so different. I didn't know why it had taken me so long to get here. I guess that stressed-out/hyped London living was all I knew.

It was my ex, Damien, who'd introduced me to Cornwall. I'd fallen in love with Damien and Cornwall – it was the package. He was from down here and as a couple, we would come on holidays to visit his family and have romantic mini-breaks in a thatched cottage on the Helford Passage. It was dreamy up to a point and I would have married him, but as the years rolled by, I realised he was married to the bottle. Drink was his mistress, not me. His Faustian bargain despair increased daily. I saw it in his eyes – the spark of life gradually going out.

But with Sam, it was a slow burn – he wasn't the big explosion into my life that Damien had been. I loved Sam more as time went by - especially when the children arrived - whereas with Damien I liked him less and less, repulsed by the constant smell of alcohol on his breath and his inability to stick to anything that resembled *work*.

Only a week before my hospital appointment, I could have ticked all the boxes – you really *could* have it all, I thought. I was also in the enviable position of writing my first novel, having been picked up by a major publishing house, which every journalist pretty much dreams of.

Was the little lump I'd found going to change all that? Does God rescue you from drowning, just to beat you up on the beach? I really had been drowning when Sophie was born. She was put into intensive care – she had to be resuscitated, a complication of her birth, I nearly lost her – my beautiful baby girl.

****

The appointment with Mr. Jones was coming to an end. 'I'm off to get a Cornish pasty, then,' I smiled weakly at him, and we left.

We left the hospital and headed towards the car park. Neither of us could think of anything to say. Sam fumbled through his jean pockets to find change for the parking machine, while I sat in the car waiting for him, wondering - why was he taking so long?

I had a pile of booklets and leaflets on my lap as if I was a fresher on a university course, but they were all about a subject I wished to know nothing about. I picked up the *Sex & Cancer* leaflet, read the contents: Feeling Attractive, Contraception, How to Relax. I crunched it into a ball and chucked it on the floor.

Contraception? Suddenly I remembered something that Bridget - the Irish nurse - had mentioned *en passant* during a 'how are you feeling?' chat before the appointment with the surgeon. But I'd been too worried about dying, to take it in. 'Make sure you're extra careful with contraception, this wouldn't be a good time to get pregnant.'

The realisation suddenly kicked in: Oh god, the other night. What had I done? We hadn't used contraception. I wasn't on the pill. It was the last thing on my mind. It wasn't so much that I didn't want another baby – we'd discussed it – but now it was out of bounds.

What if I was pregnant? If so, I couldn't have treatment, at least not radiation, and then I might die. I started manically counting and recounting days since my last period. Yes, it had been bang in the middle of my cycle. Tears started rolling down my face - how could I have been such an idiot? What was I to do now? At that moment Sam opened the driver's door, hopped in and slammed the door really hard: 'That bloody machine took my money and didn't give me my ticket back.' Oblivious to my tears and the lack of response from the passenger seat, he started the car up, whacked the gear stick into reverse and spun round at speed in the direction of the barrier. Up it went for a blue BMW, and Sam drove maniacally through just behind it. As the barrier came down, it hit the edge of our boot.

'I told you we should've got a cab,' said Sam. I was wailing now. The car park was heaving with motorists trying to leave, all eyes trained on us. We drove off, not bothering to survey the damage.

Thoughts...

Stress
The exact causes of breast cancer are largely unknown. Stress is a contributor, if you don't have time to meditate, listen to music or an uplifting podcast.

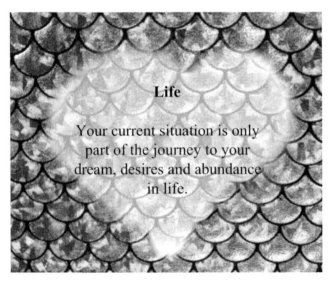

Life

Your current situation is only part of the journey to your dream, desires and abundance in life.

5: Mr. Jones

As the light faded, Dick wove down the familiar country lanes in his Aston Martin heading home. He loved this time of day it was meditative and thinking time for him. His mind sifted and sorted through the day's events. Roughly a 20-minute drive, which was perfect for this as he looped his way through the undulating countryside. Which by day was breaking into the yellows and reds of autumn before him and by night had rabbits darting out of the way to avoid being squashed. He reckoned that on the country lanes he was safer at night, the headlights of the cars coming the other way meant you could spot a car way in advance and slow down to a crawl accordingly.

He flicked on the radio - Robert Palmer's: *She Makes My Day'* was playing 'I feel so lucky loving her ...'

It had been his and Jasmine's wedding song. Dick pulled off the road, slammed on the brakes and came to a screeching halt outside a rundown farm. He was in a wide gateway leading into an empty field, there was no one around. He slumped over the steering wheel, his head in his hands, tears began tracing down his face. He stayed like this for some time - he didn't know how long for. Alone in the dark, with no lights up ahead, the cold got the better of him, he started to shiver, turning on the ignition, he cranked up the temperature of the heated leather seats and sped off, chastising himself for such weakness. He couldn't remember the last time he had cried.

Finally, he pulled up outside his elegant gated Georgian house. He and Jasmine had spent a fortune doing it up five years earlier, after they'd left their waterside apartment in Battersea with its aerial views of London, relocating to Cornwall with their two small daughters, Isobel and Mimi. Dick had been offered a new challenge: to open a state-of-the art Centre for Breast Cancer in the West Country, complete with a lucrative financial package.

As a small boy he had visited Cornwall on holiday with his parents. They didn't have a car back then, so would go by bus as his dad, a coach driver, got free travel. Every year, they would stay at the same B&B in Sennen, which paid homage to the 1970s - with pink candlewick bedspreads and swirly-patterned carpets. He had some of the happiest memories of his childhood on the beach with his mum and dad, building sandcastles and catching drips of ice cream from his 99 Flake before the sweet creamy vanilla hit the sand.

Jasmine had thrown herself into the project management of the move to the new house in Cornwall, despite the chaos of the building work, the dust and the Grade II listed planning restrictions, renovating the house had been a golden time for them as a couple. Jasmine had exquisite taste having lived all her life in fine houses. She really suited her role of Lady of the Manor, ordering builders around and making them cups of sugary tea, bacon sandwiches and flapjacks. She enjoyed poring over swatches from Designers Guild and swathes of material from West End furnishing houses. She had been in her element then, largely because she had something to do. Later, with their girls at boarding school – her choice, not Dick's – her mothering skills were only required every other weekend and during school holidays.

Dick loved coming home from work, uncorking a bottle of wine and hearing over dinner about progress on the house. Jasmine had been so animated back then. But since the house had been finished, she had gone downhill.

Dick appreciated the house's rural isolation all he could see were fields and hedgerows. Here he could escape his patients and properly relax without bumping into any of them - which wouldn't be the case if he'd been living in Truro. He needed that separation in order to give his all when he was at work.

He liked to mull over his patients in his mind – what was best for them, psychologically as well as physically. A woman who had gotten through treatment successfully and seemed positive and upbeat might be the same woman who became clinically depressed after it was all over, which of course he took as a failure on his part. Generally speaking, the women who did psychologically better were the ones that had full breast reconstruction including nipple reconstruction and tattooing to add colour – fifty shades of pink or brown.

Dick knew it was disheartening for a woman to face her body after surgery, alone, staring at the reflection in the bathroom mirror, it would be a constant reminder of the trauma she had undergone. His aim on completion of treatment was that a woman could sunbathe topless, such were his skills of oncoplastic surgery - akin to artistry in his case.

Five years on, he still had feelings of guilt and frustration over Liz Green - A former patient. No one had ever thought Liz would make it, not even him. She was a 31-year-old bookkeeper – very bright, very pretty, with two small children and an adoring husband. The younger you are - the more serious the risk of the cancer spreading, as cells are dividing at a faster rate.

Liz had a Grade 4 aggressive form of breast cancer – there isn't a Grade 5 – which had spread to her lymph nodes her prognosis was not good. Her oncologist had administered the maximum dose of chemotherapy to shrink the multiplying tumours. The dose had to be spot on – too much and it would kill her, too little and it wouldn't work - she could die.

Liz had exceeded all expectations. The tumours had shrunk down to nothing and she'd coped remarkably well with the following double mastectomy, opting for bilateral reconstruction at a later date - the doctors had been amazed by her.

She was a self-styled Joan of Arc - with a headscarf over her bald head and clothes that hung off her due to the vomit-inducing chemo. This look got her a lot of attention and sympathy from the medical profession, her friends and the public in general who would cock their head and ask: 'How are you? How's treatment going?' she would fill them in with all the gory details, leaving nothing to the imagination. She loved talking about cancer, her cancer and all aspects of it – it was as if nothing else had ever happened in her life to date.

Her Joan of Arc-look generally worked, but occasionally backfired. Post-chemo, and before Liz had reconstruction, she and her long-suffering husband went on a much-needed break to Antigua whilst the grandparents looked after their children. Liz was having hot flushes on the long flight due to the Tamoxifen she was on, so she'd stripped down to a vest top. With her bald head, flat chest and skeletal body, she resembled a twink, so much so - that one passenger on the flight - an elderly man, had said to Liz's husband, Ben, as he was queuing for the bathroom: 'If you want a man why don't you get yourself a *man*?' nodding in Liz's direction. Ben had looked at him in horror and embarrassment, said nothing and sat back down in his seat. He didn't want anyone to see his pain on hearing this remark. After all, he had held the whole family together – worked, looked after the children, taken his wife to appointments, done the housework and walked their two dogs. He'd experienced things with his wife that no man should have to go through. Yet here they were on this break, the beginning of a supposedly happier phase for them.

But it hadn't been this incident that had prompted Liz's decline. After her treatment had finished and she'd been discharged from the hospital, she started drinking. The hospital had encouraged her to have a glass of wine with dinner if she wanted to take the edge off things. But she took this to the extreme and started downing a bottle of wine a night, then two.

She had loved being centre of attention - wearing her cancer badge with pride. 'I've got cancer' opened doors for her in the way that it did if you were a minor celebrity. She had one topic of conversation – cancer and its treatment. Although the cancer support group she attended religiously each week urged her to move on. She became a woman obsessed, who'd lost interest in normality, her children and husband.

She couldn't quit drinking and she lost her job. Her despairing husband was awarded custody of their children – she was no longer capable of looking after them. It ended up that she would have a seizure if she attempted to withdraw from alcohol. But despite abusing her body, the cancer hadn't returned - although she regularly pretended that it had and would tell her children - which further infuriated her now ex-husband.

Dick knew intellectually there had been nothing more he could have done for her, but being a perfectionist, he still blamed himself for her decline, as he did for his mother's death.

His patients came in roughly three types of categories, Professional patients like Liz Green - who made a career out of cancer, and the self-styled experts like Dorothy Niels - who had swallowed a medical dictionary. But there were also the Vicky Pollards – Am I bovvered? – who just stuck their head in the sand - never questioned anything and did exactly what they were told.

But this week, Dick had met a patient who was different from all the others, she didn't fall into any of the above categories - she was unique. When he wasn't raging internally about Jasmine - she would pop into his mind now and then. He wondered about Charlotte James. She didn't have the jaw-dropping beauty of Jasmine, more the girl-next-door - she wasn't blonde. He preferred blondes, as his mother had been, but you didn't have to be a Freudian scholar to work that one out. Charlotte wasn't tiny-waisted like Jasmine either, but there was something about her that was refreshing, intriguing almost … he couldn't really put his finger on it.

Dick buzzed the electric gates open which led onto their substantial driveway, flanked on either side by landscaped gardens and the demurely manicured bay and olive trees which led down to their summer house. When they first moved in, if it was a mild evening and the children were at school, he and Jasmine would head for the den with a bottle of wine and watch the sun go down, sampling a selection of meze from Harrods' food hall or a local deli that Jasmine had found and pestered into supplying her with Middle Eastern fare. The summer house - expertly done up by Jasmine - resembled a Moroccan riad festooned in deep hues of purple, red and gold with traditional tin lights lit by candles and miniature oil burners scented with orange-blossom oil. There was a selection of large floor cushions - where they would usually end up making love. It had been their own little world, their secret bubble miles away from anyone. Nothing, he thought, could shatter the peace they had found there.

He yanked his lanyard off – he hated those damn things – chucked it on the back seat, slammed the car door and crunched his way down the wide gravel path leading to his front door.

He looked round, spotting Jasmine's new cream and black Mercedes convertible parked up in front of the double garage. This was a first, blocking both garage doors. The deal had been that he would buy her the convertible she wanted providing - she kept it in one of the garages.

But she rarely did. In a fit of anger, he punched the key fob and watched as both double garage doors opened simultaneously without making a sound. There was clearly no room to park a car in Jasmine's bay. Piled up on the concrete floor were boxes and bags of shopping: turquoise Tiffany bags, green Harrods bags and a selection of Harvey Nichols' designer carriers. None of which had been opened.

Dick looked up at the house – the third-floor bedroom was lit up whilst the rest of the house was dark. He felt another stab of disappointment – Jasmine probably wasn't preparing any dinner for them. God, all I want after a hard week - he thought to himself- was to come home to my family, have dinner and a glass or two of wine. Was that so much to ask? As he glanced back at Jasmine's car, he spotted a dent in the driver's side door – the car was only six weeks old, if that. He'd ordered the new model about a year ago and paid extra to get it for her on her birthday as a surprise. Now he wished he hadn't.

He couldn't stand it anymore. When not at work, he spent most waking moments feeling anger and disappointment at the way she was treating him. It was hurting him more than she could possibly ever know. But he didn't want to spoil the weekend as he was excited about seeing the girls who should be back from school.

The house was quiet. 'Jasmine?' he hollered up the stairs. 'Where are the girls?' Still no reply. He ran two steps at a time to the third floor, where their vast bedroom and wet room occupied the entire floor. Clothes and still more designer carrier bags, opened ones this time, were strewn on the floor, making their immaculately Farrow & Ball-muted bedroom resemble a charity shop.

He followed a narrow strip of cream carpet not covered in clothes to the bathroom door and pushed it open with his elbow. Years of time spent in hospitals had ingrained this hygiene routine in him even when it wasn't required. The bathroom was steamed up and for a moment he couldn't spot Jasmine, as she was nearly submerged under a layer of bubbles in the roll-top bath. Scented candles surrounded the bath and a fire roared in the grate. An empty champagne flute and a bar of jasmine-scented soap – her signature fragrance – balanced precariously next to the champagne glass on a small round marble table by the side of the bath.

'Darling!' she squealed. 'Have some Moet?'

Eyeing his wife's breasts, her light pink nipples poking through the foamy water, 'Where are Isobel and Mimi?' he asked calmly – his voice belying the anger he really felt, his overwhelming erection and the desire he now had to fuck her.

'Oh, they're coming tomorrow.'

'Tomorrow? But it's the weekend. We were having a family weekend – that's what we discussed.'

'They'll be here by lunchtime.'

'But weren't you were supposed to be picking them up on the way back from London? Isn't that why you went there?'

'Don't worry. Their housemistress will be putting them on the train at 9.15am and I'll collect them from the station.'

'They're going by train? They're only 10 and 12. What are you thinking of?'

'I know it's not ideal, but I got stuck getting out of London – the traffic was terrible.'

'The traffic's always terrible out of London on a Friday.'

'I wanted to get back before you and surprise you.'

Clearly not to make me any dinner, he thought but didn't say.

'I rang Mrs. Cuthbert-Smith and said I'd be late. She was so charming. It was her suggestion, not mine. She talked me into it, that they should have their supper at school as it was getting late and they could go in the morning.'

Dick knew he could play this one, or two ways. He could make it worse: have a massive row – which there had been plenty of those lately – or let it go, it was after all a done deed now. He was sick and tired of all the rowing. Maybe he could calm down – he was good at that. It was a practice he'd developed at work. If things got really stressful and busy in theatre he would slow down and breathe deeply to get his heart rate back down to a normal pace.

He started to breathe more evenly, filling the whole of his pulmonary cavity with air. They could have a nice evening – order a Chinese, maybe. He picked up her glass to pour himself a glass of champagne, but the bottle was empty.

'Get another one from downstairs.' Jasmine picked up the bar of soap, inhaled its heady mixture of essential oils – she had about 20 bars of it in the cupboard – and started soaping her breasts. 'I thought we could have some time to ourselves,' she said in her home counties accent which Dick always found such a turn-on after growing up in the rough East End. It had been such an achievement to bag a posh girl like Jasmine, he was madly in love with her and always would be. He felt she was his soulmate.

He remembered the first time he'd clapped eyes on her. He had been at medical school with her brother James, who was throwing a drinks party to celebrate his 30th birthday at their town house in Notting Hill.

Jasmine, 25, at the time, had in tow a narcissistic boyfriend - Hugo, who loved the sound of his own voice or so Dick thought. Hugo had been working in the City for a major merchant bank, no longer trading, courtesy of overinvestment in sub-prime mortgages. Dick had thought he'd had no chance with Jasmine, but he'd been wrong.

He didn't have long to wait. Two months later, James invited him to a dinner, he was seated at a table of eight guests across from the beautiful Jasmine. She'd dumped Hugo the week before. She looked like a china doll in a backless oyster-coloured satin dress that accentuated her tiny waist, and heels that gave her extra height. She kept gazing at him - a little too long across the table. It was that night he'd fallen in love with her, even though politically they were opposites. He shunned private medicine and believed firmly in state education – after all it had served him well whereas her background was Tory to the core and had been for generations in her family.

But that night, the two of them cared little for political persuasion. She didn't even ask him about his work – just knowing that he was a surgeon had been enough for her. He asked her about her life, though. She had very much been brought up, rather than dragged up like Dick. She was doing an MA in history of art at Chelsea. She told him about stints in Florence studying art at the British Institute and doing life drawing classes. She peppered the conversations with Italian phrases, which Dick found a turn-on. He had never been to Italy nor sampled scamorza or mortadella, like Jasmine, *Pinot Grigio* and spaghetti bolognese formed the extent of his knowledge of Italian gastronomy. His life until this point had pretty much been work, work and work. He'd had his head in a book since his mother had died. That night, it was as if meeting Jasmine, he was finally coming up for air.

'Money means nothing to me,' she'd confided in him when they went out onto the balcony with their cognacs to watch the pink-tinged sunset.

It was easy to say that when you've always had it all handed to you, Dick thought - but didn't say so. He was more focused on his desire to kiss her.

'What I want most in the world is to be a mother and have a large family.'

Dick was hooked. It was, after all, what he wanted too. Being an orphan with no siblings meant family was everything to him.

Over dinner he had wondered; why she'd not seemed to take time gently savouring the superb wines and pushed her food around her plate without eating it, followed by disappearing to the cloakroom several times, but he put it down to nerves. He didn't care. He was smitten with her. How could he have been anything else?

They married a year later – their castle wedding and honeymoon in St Kitts were exquisite. On their honeymoon, Dick realised he'd never been so happy. It was intoxicating. This beautiful creature was his lover, but also gave him the security his mother had given him all those years ago. He'd forgotten how good it felt.

Izzy was a honeymoon baby. Jasmine was the happiest and the most content when pregnant. Even when pregnant she was the envy of all women – looking like she'd swallowed an olive.

****

Dick's anger melted – his desire for sex was stronger than any rational thought. He ripped off his clothes, revealing a stonking erection - went over to the bath and leapt on top of Jasmine.

Her skin was so smooth and smelt divine. He slid his hands down to her breasts, and her nipples instantly hardened.

He pulled her lithe frame out of the soapy water, laying her carefully on the rug in front of the fire. With the flickering light of the flame and candles dancing around them, he gently pulled her thighs apart running his fingers lightly up the inside of her thighs towards her throbbing wet cunt, he fingered her gently whilst seducing her with his hypnotic gaze. He tried to make it last longer, but as she moaned with the pleasure of orgasm, he couldn't resist any longer, he plunged his cock deeply into her – the release was ecstatic. They both fell asleep afterwards on the soft rug by the fire, the exhaustion of the week taking its toll on him along with the champagne and hot bath rendering her unconscious.

After an hour, Dick woke up with a jolt – he was hungry. He gazed at the still sleeping Jasmine, whose chest was rising and falling in deep sleep. He scooped her up in his arms, laid her gently on the bed and tucked her in. She didn't stir.

Jasmine always seemed to have a detachment about her. Sex was the only time he really had her attention. It felt like that was all she could contribute to the relationship – her looks and the way she used them. Yet Charlotte popped into his mind again, he had *her* attention in a way that he wanted from Jasmine. Dick would notice the way other men looked at Jasmine – transfixed by those brown eyes – particularly Mountford, one of the junior doctors Dick worked closely with. Normally full of his own self-importance, Mountford couldn't string a sentence together if Jasmine was around. Secretly Dick hated Tom Mountford. Their respective upbringings couldn't have been more different. And 'Mounts', as everyone called him – a throwback to his public-school days – always had an agenda.

Dick in his moments of self-doubt, would imagine what the junior doctor was thinking – that someone as beautiful as Jasmine had only married him for his money and status. But Dick also kept his secret – Mountford wasn't very bright, he'd only just scraped into medical school despite the vast expense spent on his private education and crammer. He wasn't an instinctive doctor at all – he was more of a regurgitator of facts – his bedside manner was extremely lacking. He would often be cold and condescending to patients.

Dick was now in the difficult position of nominating the annual prize for medicine to an outstanding junior doctor at the breast cancer charity dinner - which was coming up. The event raised funds for the hospital, making up the NHS shortfall, keeping open the Centre of Excellence that Dick had built up. Without this money providing medical care fewer women would get treated and some would die. The stakes were high, he needed Jasmine on board despite their current marital difficulties, and to show a united front. Jasmine was also very well connected – her cousins were in the Cabinet. Meanwhile, Sir Hugh Mountford, the major benefactor - Tom's father - was putting huge pressure on Dick to put Tom forward for the prize: the hospital higher echelons had made it clear – no award for Mounts, no funding.

Wrapping a bath towel around his torso, Dick padded downstairs barefoot to the kitchen to make something to eat. The answer machine was flashing messages. He pressed Play: a deep, plummy voice announced: 'It's Mrs. Cuthbert-Smith here. I'm very concerned. I've tried your mobile several times. The girls are both in tears. They were expecting you to pick them up at four. It's after six now. Please call as soon as you can. The girls are worried you've had an accident. We're all worried.'

Dick pressed Redial instantly: 'It's Richard Jones here. Isobel and Mimi's dad,' he heard himself saying to their housemistress. 'I'm so sorry to call you at this late hour and for the position we've put you in. Jasmine was taken ill, but please tell the girls she's fine now and sleeping. I'll get up at six tomorrow morning and come and collect them myself.'

Thoughts...

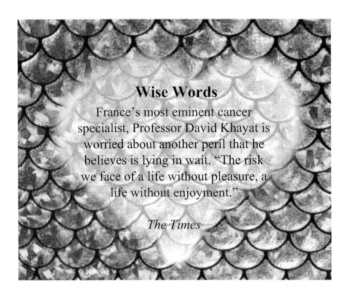

Wise Words

France's most eminent cancer specialist, Professor David Khayat is worried about another peril that he believes is lying in wait. "The risk we face of a life without pleasure, a life without enjoyment."

The Times

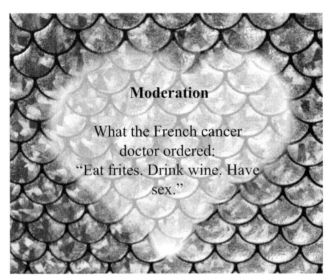

Moderation

What the French cancer doctor ordered: "Eat frites. Drink wine. Have sex."

6: Charlotte

I was feeling low and vulnerable, so I called the hospital for reassurance, 'Go out and get some fresh air,' Nurse Tough Love (aka Bridget Mary Woods or BMW) had said down the end of the phone. 'Don't sit around getting miserable indoors – you'll feel worse.'

I hugely admired BMW, her Irishness, her sparkly mischievous eyes and humour. I would do anything she said, it was her subject. I didn't know a thing about breast cancer – didn't want to.

So, I decided to make beef casserole and mash for dinner - as eating comfort food might make things better. I headed to the butchers round the corner – the butcher was carving a large rack of meat; I felt as though his knife was cutting into my chest neatly separating fleshy breast and nipple from my ribcage. There was no blood, no pain, just the sensation of the shiny metal blade doing its work. Then there was an unmistakable cracking sound as he severed each rib, one-by-one.

I hurled my entire body weight at the door and stumbled to a nearby bin, held my hair back and was violently sick. I sank to the ground, wiping the drool from my face. Composing myself for a few minutes, I figured that sitting against the wall of the butcher's shop was a better option than the bin, and besides, wafts of rotting meat as well as sick were coming my way. I hauled myself up and staggered back.

The shop door sprung open a young student came out clutching a white carrier bag containing a paper package bulging with ribs. Fortunately, he didn't notice me. Instead, he headed down the hill – towards an excited dog being unleashed from a lamp post. But coming up the hill behind me was someone who really would notice me judging by his self-satisfied grin, already had.

'Charlotte.'

'Damien,' I said weakly.

'Why are you sitting on the ground like a hobo? Is that sick I can smell? I've told you about your drinking.'

'I thought you were in London?' I replied.

****

Splitting up with Damien – the heartbreak had been immeasurable. It was as if each of my limbs were being torn off one-by-one - the pain was physical. It was November, I just couldn't get warm no matter what I did. My life would never be as bleak, or would it?

The day I'd met Damien, my world had changed from monochrome to colour. Looking back, I was so ripe for it. Damien was about ten years older than me, but because of the alcoholism, he looked a good fifteen or twenty years older. He was very much the older man - always telling me what to do and what not to do, which for a while suited me perfectly. But for him, drink was a poison which tainted everything in his life.

Damien also had the fortune or misfortune to be the brother of Jack Rashleigh, who had - on the surface of it - a meteoric rise to godlike celebrity status with his TV show, known as the JR Show, which spotted young talent. He would saunter onto the set to the signature sound of *T-Rex's Dandy of the Uunderworld* with the widest grin on his face.

It could have been so different - if it hadn't been for Jack. Even before his fame, Damien had been envious – actually, envious isn't the right word, he was jealous, jealous as hell of the brother who was ten years younger than him. But rather than admit his own failings, he was just in Jack's shadow the whole time. Not facing up to who he was – i.e., not Jack Rashleigh, 'The Rash' as he was known, largely for his rash remarks and rapier-like wit.

The thing about Jack Rashleigh and Damien, was that they had different fathers. Damien's father - Arthur Scrace - had been a drinker and had absconded when Damien was a baby. Damien had been put in a children's home until his mother - Molly - remarried several years later and had another child so took him out of the orphanage. Whereas the stunningly handsome Jack had everything money could buy while he was growing up – private school, the big houses in London and Cornwall. Whilst Damien had suffered the indignity of being nicknamed 'orphan boy' at school.

Damien wouldn't admit that he had a drink problem - this was his downfall. If he'd just come out and admitted it, things could have been a lot different. But his pride wouldn't let him. He was the alcoholic who couldn't stop drinking, who didn't have any money and would rather spend a sunny afternoon in a grotty pub than be with me.

The drink made everything better for him, well… for the time being. Damien would rather be drunk than sober. Because being drunk was better than having the thoughts that were in his head, thoughts of self-hatred, self-loathing, which you would never guess upon meeting him. He was such a flamboyant, funny, out-there character. Only those close to Damien – not even Jack – knew the truth. 'Just have one,' Jack would say, 'like me.' But Damien couldn't have just one drink. One drink was the equivalent of eating one peanut. Who can eat one peanut? No one can, can they?

In spite of all of this, when I was a young 20-something, upon meeting him, I had no idea about alcohol. I didn't go to pubs. I didn't particularly like drinking. It was only when I got older that I discovered wine and the benefits of it, particularly after the children had been put to bed. But even then, I wouldn't have more than two glasses.

Damien's despair got worse the more he didn't face up to it. He was the classic Jekyll and Hyde: one minute lovely, the next cruel. He did love me, but he loved the drink more. The alcohol was his mistress, the drink was more enticing than me. He really did try to stop drinking, but he couldn't – the memories of what he had been through as a child kept haunting him. He had been a gangly child who at teatime would have to watch a stout matron finish off the butter whilst he had dry bread. Visiting times, once a fortnight, were the worst. The children had to put on their Sunday best and wait for their parents to arrive. Invariably, Molly couldn't make it as she earnt her living in show business and usually would be on tour in another part of the country. Damien was always the last child left waiting in the room. The sound of heels walking away on parquet flooring still haunted him.

****

We had this schizophrenic existence where we'd fly off to LA. Jack would pay for the tickets, send the limo, we would stay at Jack's mansion in Beverly Hills and he would pay for everything. It's really different if you know someone before fame. The thing about Jack was, that he always thought he was famous, so it was no surprise to him, given it was his birth right. He had that confidence from his mother and the love she had given him as a child. She had been there for him and believed in him. Molly had been very young when she had Damien.

These were the family secrets which had been kept well hidden from everyone. All Jack had known was that Damien was the black sheep of the family. He was always in trouble, always in debt, and drank far too much causing mayhem. Jack didn't know what had gone on in Damien's past to make him like this.

I fell madly in love with Damien, he made me laugh, and laugh a lot - flipside, he made me cry. The saddest thing about Damien and I, was just that we couldn't be together – it made him really sad. Damien knew he was destroying the relationship but he couldn't do anything about it. I think I reminded him of his mother, he had so much anger towards her and he projected it onto me. I even resembled her when she was younger. Many years after she'd passed away, I'd kept a black and white framed photo of her from a show on my mantelpiece, and when my daughter she was very little she pointed to it and said: 'Mama?'

I'd had first met Daniel when I was a young trainee reporter in London. I'd gone to do an interview with the author of a book about stress - at the Kensington Gardens Hotel, close to Kensington Palace – In walked Damien, he purported to be a writer's agent, but possibly he was just trying to get money out of him. The minute he walked in the sun came out. It really was that cliché.

They were innocent days back then. No terrorist attacks in the City, no pandemics and no one had heard of Jack Rashleigh. He was just an unsung star in the world of entertainment. I hadn't known of Jack Rashleigh's existence until I met Damien. Rashleigh wasn't even Damien's real surname. He was really Andrew Damien Scrace. Damien thought it was hilarious that his initials sounded like A Disgrace, but when Jack started his ascent to stardom, Damien changed his name to Rashleigh, so he wasn't really a Rashleigh at all.

I had been dating someone that I met when I was at university, but he was nothing special. Whereas Damien was very special. It was a pivotal moment in my life - which way was I going to go with this? I could have settled down with my boyfriend after Uni, but I didn't. I was pulled like a magnet and there was no way I could stop this relationship from happening. I thought I had found my soulmate – but the thing about soulmates was, that they're just there to hurt you and to teach you lessons before you meet the right person. They're not necessarily the romantic partner that you hope for. But Damien was funny, really funny. He was similar to Jack in that way. It must have been genetic they both had the showman in them.

I had problems too, I just didn't do the drink thing. But my reaction to his drinking was seismic; this made matters worse.

****

When Damien spotted me outside the butcher's, I thought it wouldn't be a good idea to break down and tell him I had breast cancer. A few years ago or so, he'd left a message on my voicemail – after he'd been drinking, of course saying 'My mother's dying and you don't even care.' His mother had a scare on finding a breast lump but it had turned out to be benign.

Damien surveyed me and said: 'You seem to have lost some weight, which isn't a bad thing, so keep it up, whatever you're doing.' For as long as I could remember, Damien had always been obsessed with my weight, he routinely tried to stop me eating certain things. His brother Jack was always surrounded by model types and generally over-thin women. I felt huge next to them despite my normal body weight. I remember one trip to LA, staying at Jack's mansion and lying in the garden sunbathing in a bikini. Having substantial thighs I was worried that some photographer would catch a picture of me, from a low-flying aeroplane and there would be a headline running the next day: *'The Rash has Found Himself a Fatty'* because I weighed in at nine and a half stone rather than seven stone something, which was more the norm with LA stick insects.

The shock of being told I had breast cancer, rapidly knocked half a stone off my frame. I was on the Mr. Jones diet he could tell any woman the same thing and they'd lose weight. I pulled myself up, said goodbye to Damien, and headed back home. When I got in, my answer machine was flashing. I pressed Play.

'Hi darling, it's Selina here. Just to let you know, we're pulling that piece on breast cancer. Apparently, breast cancer is *so* last week. We want a new different cancer to lead with. Can you cobble together a story with a group of case studies with new, exciting forms of cancer? How are you by the way? I haven't heard from you for a while.'

I slammed the delete button.

Thoughts...

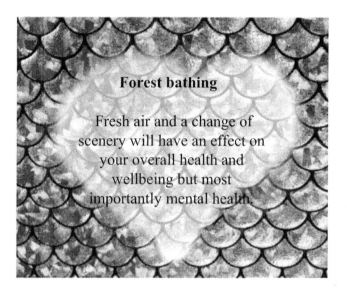

Forest bathing

Fresh air and a change of
scenery will have an effect on
your overall health and
wellbeing but most
importantly mental health.

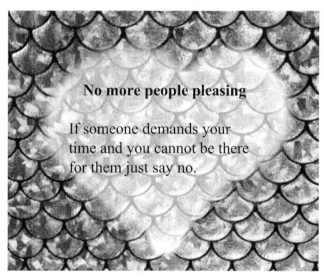

No more people pleasing

If someone demands your
time and you cannot be there
for them just say no.

7: Mr. Jones

It was the night of the May charity ball. Dick was feeling optimistic, almost excited about the evening. Things between him and Jasmine seemed to be improving; she hadn't drunk for three weeks, and it was as if she and Dick were on their honeymoon again. Certainly, the sex was non-stop - he felt like the luckiest man in Cornwall.

It was really important that the night would go well in order to secure resourcing for the new unit. Dick was feeling quietly confident that Sir Hugh Mountford would be pleased with the plan for the hospital expansion. The only thing that irked Dick - that really went against the grain - was the fact that he was having to award Tom Mountford the prize for 'Best Breast Cancer Doctor'. The deal – or rather the bribe – was that Sir Hugh's son would get the honour and glory, meaning Sir Hugh would come up with the financing. Dick felt he had no choice, the NHS cuts meant the more independent funding they got, the more people they could treat and potentially save. But Tom was not the gifted and talented doctor his father had been.

****

Jasmine came out of the shower looking dewy with damp tousled hair, padding around barefoot whilst she selected dress-after-dress from her walk-in wardrobe - discarding each of them on the bed in a pile of expensive fabric - with a creamy concoction on top of the pile. 'What do you think,'

'What about the cream lace number?'

'You mean the shift dress?'

'Uh, yeah.'

Her towel dropped to the floor, but Dick decided that as much as he wanted to, it was not the moment. The girls were on the next floor doing their homework and a babysitter was arriving imminently. He and Jasmine needed to leave shortly, in order to get there on time for this evening to be a success.

The limo dropped them outside the Cathedral. Mr. Jones looked striking, stepping out in his black tie followed by Jasmine - her cream lace dress was the perfect choice. Before entering the building, he caught sight, of a brand-new Jaguar reversing into a disabled parking space. As he looked more closely, he saw the car number plate BOOBDOC. In the driver's seat was Tom Mountford looking very pleased with himself. Mr. Jones smiled and linked arms with Jasmine.

The cathedral was beautifully lit, warm and inviting, with three grand spires thrusting skywards.

The band had just started up, playing Nina Simone's: *My Baby Just Cares for Me* as Mr. Jones sauntered in with Jasmine - all eyes on her - parading the pink (rather than red) carpet, which spanned the length of the nave. The theme, naturally, was breast cancer. The pews had been removed and replaced with round tables - festooned with pink ribbons and garlands of pink gerberas. The evening kicked off with the usual speeches, Sir Hugh droning on about the importance of funding. Dick winced at Sir Hugh's reference, of how proud he was over the choice of this year's prize for most promising doctor in the field of breast cancer care.

During the three-course meal, Dick watched Jasmine like a hawk - hoping she was going to stay sober. That was going to be the biggest challenge of the evening. He made small talk to various other medics and their spouses on his table. Fortunately, he was on a different table from his student Melissa. She kept shooting him glances, which he ignored, but he was secretly amused because she and Jasmine appeared to be wearing the same dress – except that Jasmine's dress was haute couture whilst Melissa's was a copy, probably from New Look. Jasmine, observed Dick, looked classy with her slim hourglass figure and rounded breasts. But Melissa's dress couldn't conceal her bulges and did nothing to flatter her figure.

Dick watched as Tom Mountford kept finding excuses to come over to their table; but really his motive was to chat to Jasmine. She was charming in return, seeming oblivious to the effect she was having on him. She was, however, used to plenty of male attention. She had grown up with it. By the age of 12 she had always been referred to as 'the beautiful Jasmine'.

It was getting on towards the end of the evening; Dick was keen to get home, but they had to wait for the grand finale, the awards ceremony. He was tiring from all the handshakes and small talk. Jasmine had gone to the Ladies but was taking her time. After about 20 minutes, Dick started to feel twitchy. He was trying to convince himself that she was just re-applying her make-up and doing her hair for the umpteenth time rather than drinking vodka from a bottle secreted in her handbag in some corner of the cathedral. Finally, he couldn't wait any longer and went off to find her.

The corners, nooks and crannies of the cathedral were dimly lit. Dick wandered down in the direction of the chancel, when he noticed out of the corner of his eye - a couple entwined. The flickering candlelight and the cavernous shadows made it difficult for him to work out exactly what was going on. As he looked closer, he saw what looked like Melissa - with her cream lace shift dress riding up her thighs, her back pressed against the wall – and Tom Mountford fucking her.

Dick couldn't help but be amused, as he knew it was really Jasmine that Tom wanted. Dick was clearly the lucky one. How low can you go? He thought having sex in a church of all places. Melissa swigged from a bottle with one hand, whilst using the other hand to grab Tom's arse and thrust him hard into her. Dick had seen her outside the cathedral, puffing away on a cigarette, when he and Jasmine had arrived. He thought that was tacky enough but then most medics were notoriously unhealthy due to the extreme pressure of the long hours they had to work. Half the surgeons he worked with would huddle at the back of the hospital building either smoking or vaping in the rain.

As he turned to go, he heard a familiar cut-glass voice gasping, 'Oh Tom!' and realised that the woman was not Melissa. He felt a sickening stab in the solar plexus. But then he heard Sir Hugh starting on the mic, Dick knew he had to go back to present the prize and make the speech. He managed somehow to walk back through the cathedral to the microphone positioned at the front of the audience. Out of the corner of his eye, he saw Jasmine and Tom skulking back to their tables.

Sir Hugh was announcing his name: 'And now we shall raise our glasses, I would like to ask the eminent breast surgeon, Mr. Richard Jones, to give the award to this year's most promising breast cancer doctor.'

Dick paused for a moment, looked around at the audience and said in a confident voice, 'I would like to present this award to the most talented doctor we've possibly ever had in the last decade.'

He looked back at Sir Hugh, who looked confused for a moment. Mr. Jones continued: 'Could we have a big round of applause for Aalia Abraham, for Breast Cancer Doctor of the Year? Let's raise our glasses to Aalia.'

Aalia looked startled as she clambered to her feet and came up to receive a hug from Mr. Jones and a handshake from a thunderous-looking Sir Hugh.

****

On Monday morning, Dick was summoned to Sir Hugh's office. As he walked through the door… Sir Hugh yelled: 'What the hell's going on? I've pulled the funding. No new unit. I can't believe you did that to my son!'

'Your son, Sir Hugh, is fucking my wife.'

Thoughts...

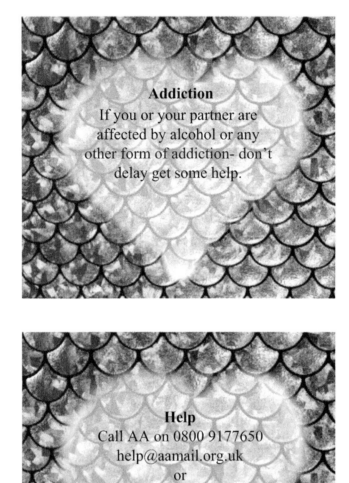

Addiction
If you or your partner are
affected by alcohol or any
other form of addiction- don't
delay get some help.

Help
Call AA on 0800 9177650
help@aamail.org.uk
or
0800 0086811
helpline@al-anonuk.org.uk

8: Charlotte

The reality of being a working mother of small children ... I did everything badly, because I had so much to do, it couldn't be any other way. I couldn't tick every box with a big black tick – it was always a small grey half-tick. My *modus operandi* was, if a job was worth doing, it was worth doing badly. I'd written articles about the importance of 'Me Time' to avoid mummy burnout. I'd often fantasised about lying in a hospital bed, all responsibility taken from me, being able to sleep eight hours a night. No meals to prepare. No deadlines. No stressed editor on my case. No kids with chicken pox. No elderly parents to worry about. No husband using me as a sounding board for every care and worry. No friends needing air time, on top of that, all the effort and personal care you have to put in to not look half-crazy. No wonder I'd got breast cancer.

When I'd done all of the above, Sam would eye me up and say 'When are you going to have a haircut?' or 'Your roots are coming through,' or 'Can you hold your stomach in?' when we were having sex. The idea of being in hospital seemed bliss.

But it was a case of be careful what you wish for in reality, you don't get any sleep on a hospital ward either. The interrogating strip lighting doesn't go off until after 11pm. After all the screaming from the patients - who can't hack the anti-coagulant injection, known as the bee sting, which is administered last thing at night to avoid DVT – is finished. Women who suffer the bee sting worse are usually those who have never had children. One 40-something woman, screamed particularly badly one night. It was so loud, even from the ward next door, that I shouted, 'It's a boy! It's a boy!' Plus, the reality of lying in a hospital bed, with a plastic duvet case sticking to your legs, being served stewed tea and hospital meals, so ghastly, that I couldn't bear to take off the metal plate cover because of the stench of the food - which heightens the nausea.

I was also in horror of what was going to happen next, no amount of positive thinking could talk me up. I didn't expect my life to be like this – in my screenplay, I didn't include these scenes of death, dying and orphaned children.

I had also done a deal with God – well, subconsciously anyway – that if I gave up Damien and the London scene - all would be well. In my script, I would live happily ever after in Cornwall, married to Sam with two beautiful kids. I would re-invent myself into a yoga-practising freelance writer cum chilled-out available mum, who wasn't tired all the time.

But all was not well, the stakes were really high now, perhaps insurmountable. It was all about balance, but I hadn't the slightest clue about what balance was.

Thoughts...

Positive thinking

Change your thoughts, and
you will change your life.

The Secret.

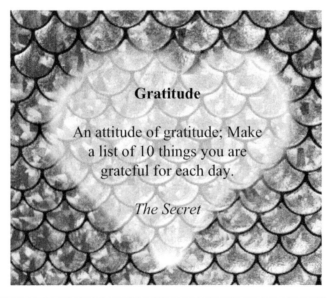

Gratitude

An attitude of gratitude; Make
a list of 10 things you are
grateful for each day.

The Secret

9: Charlotte

'I'm afraid it's not good news,' said Mr. Jones, looking intently at me. 'You have seven tumours. It's Grade 3. I've rechecked and rechecked again with the lab, that's why I've kept you waiting.'

Sam, looking very pale, edged out of the room to get some air.

I was shaking and wishing Sam hadn't gone. Mr. Jones took my hand and looked into my eyes, he said: 'We can make you better. We treat hundreds of women each year, just like you. The great news is, it hasn't gone to your lymph glands, so your prognosis is good.'

'But how come I've had seven tumours and they haven't already spread?'

'You can have one Grade 1 tumour that goes everywhere – but I guess you've been lucky.'

Lucky, I thought to myself, I'm not feeling lucky. I felt the familiar period pain and thought, I could be lucky.

'You might want to consider having a bilateral mastectomy for medical reasons, although some women find it's hard to get their head around removing a healthy breast.'

'That's not what I can't get my head around, it's the thought of dying.'

'Good answer. You're not going to die, not if I've got anything to do with it,' he said, with a gentle smile appearing on his face.

Thoughts...

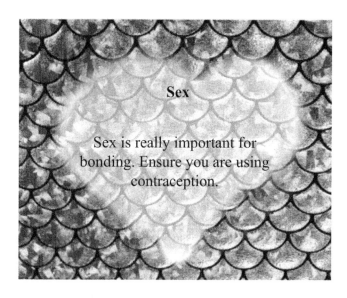

Sex

Sex is really important for bonding. Ensure you are using contraception.

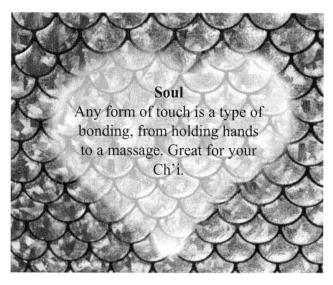

Soul
Any form of touch is a type of bonding, from holding hands to a massage. Great for your Ch'i.

10: Mr. Jones

Dick and Jasmine remained in silence for the duration of the taxi ride from the Cathedral back home and Dick slept in the guest bedroom. Then he spent all of Sunday holed up in the summer house. Since the award ceremony, he had barely exchanged a word with Jasmine about what he had seen. Fortunately, the girls had been taken back to school by one of the school mums, so he didn't have to put on a charade for the children, making out that everything was okay.

After putting down the phone to Jasmine, Uncle Monty phoned Dick. Jasmine had always been Monty's favourite, and she, tear-stained and repentant, had relayed to him the news about the financial fallout from the disastrous award ceremony. Monty normally had more money than sense, and very much enjoyed the role of benefactor, so Jasmine and he had brokered a deal that, he would put up the funding for the medical wing - on the condition that Jasmine would go into rehab for her drinking.

****

Dick went in search of his fellow surgeon, Aktor Khan. Outside of surgery hours he was usually to be found vaping if he wasn't in the hospital. Aktor, who hadn't seen Dick since Saturday night, gave his colleague a hug.

'What's the word on the street?' said Dick.

'You now have a nickname.'

'What?'

'Lady Di.'

'Lady Di?'

'Yes, because everyone loves you apart from your spouse.'

'Oh god. I don't want to get killed in a car crash.'

He thought back to a few weeks earlier. It was the day after he had signed off his medical student Melissa's progress report. He was flattering about her capabilities, as he knew that if he was anything less, she would do him for sexual harassment. The next day, as he went back into the examination room when everyone had gone home, Melissa was sitting bolt upright on the couch lying in wait for him. She pulled her top up to reveal her bouncing naked breasts. 'Why don't you lock the door, Mr. Jones?'

****

"Hello, Mountford here." I was thinking, old boy: how do you fancy playing a war doctor and disappearing for a couple of months? I've just received a call from the Red Cross Med Council out in Afghanistan saying, they need help with specialist wound healing. In light of your recent *contretemps*, I thought you'd be just the man.'

'Hugh, give me 10 minutes.' Dick ended the call.

The image of himself as a war doctor appealed to him. His girls were away at school, Jasmine was in a treatment centre and he could easily suspend all non-urgent surgery and clear the lists. The only nagging doubt was Charlotte, but he could sort something. If ever there was a time to go, it was now.

Eleven minutes later, Dick rang back: 'Hugh, I'm in.'

Thoughts...

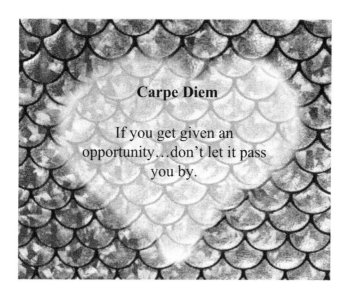

Carpe Diem

If you get given an opportunity...don't let it pass you by.

Open Up
If you or your partner are struggling to cope check out: Mandown-cornwall.co.uk or your local support group.

11: Charlotte

The day of my operation was fast approaching. It was the Friday before Prince William and Kate got married. I made the sad and lonely journey, driving myself to the hospital at 6 o'clock in the morning. It was a practical decision, as Sam needed to get the kids off to school. I also didn't want to be fussed over. I didn't like fuss. I didn't want to drag anyone out of bed. I just wanted to make it as neat an operation as possible - excuse the pun - I wasn't in the best frame of mind. As I lay in bed in my hospital gown with the curtains drawn. I felt really lost and disconnected, I picked up my phone as it went off – a message from Sam with a picture of the children - they were both dressed up for a royal wedding day party at school, they looked so unbelievably cute, their innocent smiles and bright eyes. Tears started rolling down my face. The overriding feeling was that I was a failure, a fucking failure. I'd let them down. I'd got breast cancer - It just wasn't fair.

Moments later in strode Mr. Jones, after the formalities of paperwork and consent forms, took out his marker pen to road-map my breasts. He said, 'Think of your favourite place,' but my mind was just blank. I couldn't think of anything apart from, how ludicrous my situation was. I was lost for words.

I noticed Mr. Jones's hand was shaking.

Later, lying on a trolley - adjacent to theatre - just before the anaesthetic kicked in, he whispered in my ear: 'Any final requests?'

I said: 'Kate Winslet.'

And then I woke up, woozy from anaesthetic. I was too frightened to move or pull back the gown to survey my chest, I felt revulsion for the bloodied drain, which was embedded like a circular metal toy snake in my left breast, draining off fluid. I was more or less okay, though, until I saw the pouches of blood, not realising what they were. As soon as I caught sight of it, I started hyperventilating and had to put on an oxygen mask. Each pouch was neatly hidden by an attractive fabric bag which, previously when I saw other women on the ward sporting the same bag(s) I thought it was some kind of Cath Kidston fashion statement - instead of hiding something quite medical.

Nurse Tough Love, Bridget, had warned me that Mr. Jones used copious amounts of gaffer tape – or rather surgical tape in medical terms – but now I was worried as I couldn't see much tape encasing my chest. I took a second look down, all I could see was normal-looking breasts, encased in minimal surgical tape. They couldn't have done the operation, everything looked fine from what I could see. They must have found more cancer and thought it wasn't worth doing reconstruction at that moment. Mr. Jones and his registrar, Sarah, appeared at the foot of my bed.

'Why didn't you do the operation?' I said to Mr. Jones.

'We did,' he replied.

'But there's no gaffer tape.'

'You were starting to wake up, so I didn't have time to use any more.'

I sank back into the starchy pillow in relief. I wasn't going to die after all. The anaesthetic was still working its way round my system.

Then I asked him if he'd known what I'd meant when I'd said Kate Winslet.

He said 'Of course – but was that Kate Winslet circa 2002 or Kate Winslet 2007 postpartum?'

And then I heard myself say to him: 'So, are you an East End boy made good then?'

And he said: 'Yeah, I'm from Hackney.'

'Do you carry a knife?'

'Only when I'm working.'

They both laughed, and Sarah said: 'Mr. Jones doesn't carry knives.'

Thoughts...

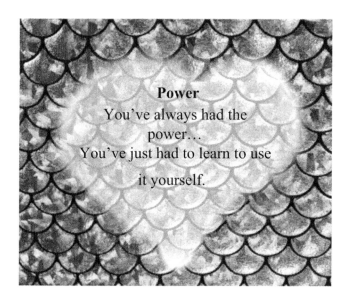

Power
You've always had the
power...
You've just had to learn to use

it yourself.

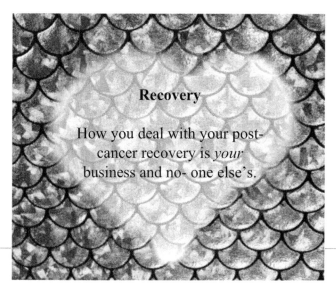

Recovery

How you deal with your post-
cancer recovery is *your*
business and no- one else's.

12: Mr. Jones

Two days later, Mr. Jones was pacing up and down the corridor, raking his hands through his hair. He needed to smuggle a patient onto the women's overspill ward - without attracting too much attention.

He'd met Ali/Alistair six months ago, when he'd first come to see him. Alistair, 26, had known since he was a child that he was in the wrong body. He wanted to transition to a man, and after a long conversation with Mr. Jones in clinic, he said:

'I want you to give me a bi-lateral mastectomy.'

'I'm sorry I can't help you, it's not a matter of life or death.'

'It is a matter of life or death,' Alistair had replied, before breaking down.

Mr. Jones handed him a tissue, and wasn't sure whether to hold his hand as he would do with his female patients in distress - but he did anyway.

Two suicide attempts and a botched double mastectomy abroad, Alistair was back for corrective surgery.

A transitioning man on the breast cancer ward, might be a bridge too far for some of the older ladies and patients when they are going through something as breast cancer. They don't always react in the same way, thought Mr. Jones.

'I might have guessed it,' said Mr. Jones as he spotted Alistair and Charlotte in the visitors' room.

'You two finding each other.'

'He's my new best friend.'

'I can see that.'

'He's also my patient who I've been looking for the last half hour and chastising BMW, Bridget Mary Woods, over this.'

'Ok, no fighting over me,' said Alistair.

Thoughts...

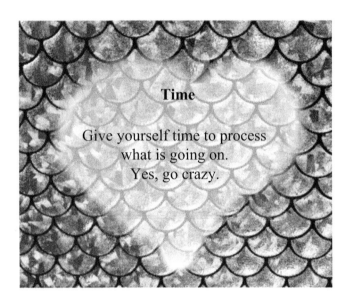

Time

Give yourself time to process
what is going on.
Yes, go crazy.

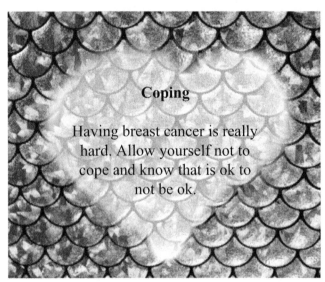

Coping

Having breast cancer is really
hard. Allow yourself not to
cope and know that is ok to
not be ok.

13: Charlotte

Spending hours alone in a hospital bed - staring at the pale ceiling of the ward - gave me a chance to think reflectively, whether I wanted to or not.

There was a right way and a wrong way of dealing with Damien; I had chosen the latter. It was only with hindsight that I realised this, but then I only got an inkling to begin with. It was after meeting Sam and having kids - that I got a vague idea of where I'd gone wrong. This resulted in me messing up the relationship with the 'big love of my life'. The thing about alcoholics is, that you can't control their drinking or what they do. I'd thought that because I wanted him to give up the alcohol, he would want to do that too - but he didn't. Even though he said he did. In better times, he would say that he was really serious about giving it up, that he wanted to get married and have children. We even booked the hotel for the wedding - St Just on the Roseland, the canapés and champagne, and chartered a yacht down to St. Mawes as an alternative to a limo.

When Damien got drunk, he would cry for his mother. It was a very difficult situation, as half of me wanted to comfort him, but then the other half didn't. He was taking it out on me. I hadn't left him in a children's home, but I was often the target of his aggression. If his brother hadn't been Jack Rashleigh, I don't even know whether it would have made any difference or whether he would have drunk anyway. But having a brother with such almost-godlike-fame, certainly made Damien's situation much harder for him to bear.

As Miss Fixit, I made him an appointment with the top addiction counsellor in London, and to please me, he went to see him. The counsellor was a red-haired Scottish guy called Iain, who had celebrity clients who had managed to stop drinking or pill popping with him. The first time he met Damien, at his clinic in Harley Street, he picked up an empty beer glass and said in his broad accent, 'You 'ain't gonna get what you want unless you put this down,' and banged the beer glass down on the desk. More than anything, Damien wanted his own TV show. Iain spelled it out to him, 'You're not gonna get your own TV show, you're not gonna get anything worthwhile, - if you carry on drinking.'

Damien came back all buoyant, having agreed to see Iain once a week. He also made a list of what he wanted to do. As well as get married and have kids, he wanted to contribute financially. Despite Jack's enormous wealth, Damien was penniless, so I, as a junior reporter, was financing him - which I deeply resented. Damien even put on the list that he wanted to help with the housework, which was touching.

Damien and I would often come to blows about finances, because he would suddenly announce, for example, *'Let's go to LA and stay at Jack's mansion. Jack says he'll pay for the tickets.'* I felt uncomfortable because, every month I would mention the mortgage payment on the flat, that I was paying and he would say, 'Oh, pend that this month.' But I couldn't get the bank to suspend it, so payments were still coming out of my account.

Damien maintained the idea of finding an agent in LA, or state that he wasn't going to come back without one. So, I found myself in LA - even though Damien didn't have his share of the gas bill to give me.

****

The first time I met Jack Rashleigh - or rather nearly met him - I legged it. Damien and I had gone for drinks at a swanky hotel in Piccadilly. I'd come straight from work, and I was so excited to see Damien that I didn't want to meet his brother, and have to make polite conversation. Not that anyone made polite conversation with Jack.

Jack was staying in the hotel with his girlfriend, Chloe, as his house in Chelsea was being renovated. Chloe was in the bar drinking, a bottle of champagne on her own. Celebrating her latest purchases courtesy of Jack from Harvey Nichols, whilst lapping up the attention from, the young waiters and embracing her recently acquired boob job – paid for by Jack of course – which was being shown off beautifully by her low-cut dress. Chloe went on to earn more money than most girls could ever dream of. After splitting with Jack, she received £5k a month as a retainer from him. He liked to keep his friends close. Damien's mother would comment on how loyal Chloe had always been, not selling her story to the newspapers - little did she know.

Damien introduced me to Chloe. Even I found myself drawn to look at her beautifully augmented breasts. But then Damien and I did a runner before Jack came down to the bar. Jack was at that time the unsung hero of the entertainment world, soon to have a meteoric rise. I can still hear my heels clacking against the marble floor of the hotel, Damien giggling with me as we made our escape.

When I eventually did meet Jack, in his mum's kitchen in Fowey, despite his usual entourage of perfectly formed beautiful model types, he seemed to recognise that I was genuine. He remarked to Damien, 'She's fantastic, she's so intelligent, she's so Mrs. D.' And I *was* so Mrs. D.

Standing in Jack's bedroom in LA, I felt overwhelmed by the stench of cigarette smoke. Jack was never without a fag in his mouth, in fact, there was always smoke coming from him. I wanted to get a bucket of water and throw it over him. Despite the beautiful monochrome bedroom, with matching his and hers en suite bathrooms, I couldn't stand the smell of cigarette smoke; I realised that even if I was with Jack, I would be nagging him constantly to give up smoking. Just as I was always nagging Damien to give up drinking. Not that Jack would push over the bevy of beautiful models to blaze a path to my door. I also didn't understand the indoor smoking thing. Because, in LA, it was always warm, so you could smoke outside in the lush manicured gardens. It wasn't like the freezing cold rain you get outside some ubiquitous London office block.

At Jack's hacienda-style mansion - complete with ornate pool and opulent gardens set in the Hollywood hills - the most impressive thing for me was the extensive range of fruit in his giant fruit bowl: papayas and pineapples and guavas and every other fruit orgasm you could ever imagine. I had serious fruit envy, but was not even remotely interested in his fleet of high-end cars such as Maseratis and Aston Martins. What I thought was his most prized possession, wasn't an SRV in fact, but his Filipino maid, Josephine, who would leave me an exquisite fruit smoothie, freshly prepared on my bedside table every morning.

Josephine had a twin sister who also worked for Jack, but in London. On one occasion, after following up some story about the latest weight loss miracle, my interview had finished early and Damien had called to say he was at Jack's. I was only round the corner. I rang Jack's doorbell, and the familiar tones of Andrew Scott's iconic dance *Dandy of the underworld* by T.Rex, came belting out over the intercom, as two metal gates swished open. It was this track, which was to become the opening credits of the JR Show. Jack would saunter onto the set, with the biggest grin and all the audience would laugh and cheer because the lyrics were just so Jack. Everyone loved The Rash.

We had Jack's London house to ourselves except for the maid. Damien had tried to persuade me to have sex with him in Jack's bed, laughing that I could do a story on romping in Jack Rashleigh's bed. I declined the bed - not the sex. During a moment of intense passion with Damien on the sofa, my editor rang me, saying 'Where the hell are you, Charlotte?' After delving down the back of the sofa, and running around the house I realised that I had misplaced my knickers, and had to return to work. But unbeknown to me, the maid was so thorough with her cleaning that she had picked them up off the floor, washed and steamed them, and they were airing in the utility room. I managed to scramble back into them and get back to work just in time. My editor had left several messages on my mobile, asking where I was. I didn't tell him about being at Jack Rashleigh's house, because I knew, he would set on me to drag salacious gossip story on Jack, and I didn't want to betray Damien.

Thoughts...

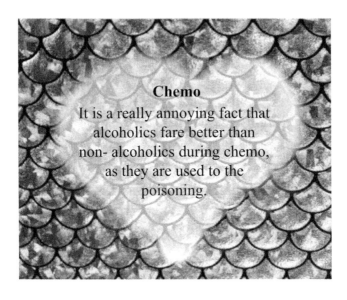

Chemo
It is a really annoying fact that alcoholics fare better than non- alcoholics during chemo, as they are used to the poisoning.

Watered down
As for drinking during chemo, I could barely drink water never mind alcohol.

14: Mr. Jones

It was Saturday night and Mr. Jones was downstairs pacing the wooden floor. He didn't know what to do. Jasmine had gone into rehab – she was expected to be there for at least three months and the girls were at sleepovers. Mr. Jones had rarely spent any time on his own, he was either at work or doing family stuff. Whilst others crave solitude and a bit of peace and quiet, Mr. Jones always kept himself busy, although after a day spent in theatre, particularly if it was hard going, he would often feel really flat after the hype and adrenaline rush of surgery. And now Aktor Kahn had invited him to an Indian restaurant to celebrate his birthday with his family.

Mr. Jones really valued his friendship with Aktor, but he felt it was difficult spending time around other people's family when you didn't have your own, and having to put on a front. He didn't want to be the misery around the table of happy people. But this was the first time in fifteen years that he'd spent any real time away from Jasmine, the smell of perfume still lingering in the bedroom wrenched him back to the time just after his mother had died, when he could smell Elizabeth Arden in her room. It was the same feeling of loss and abandonment, was he losing Jasmine now too? Losing her to the bottle and Harvey Nichols? He decided to accept Aktor's invitation.

As Mr. Jones pushed open the door of the Bombay Brasserie he was blasted with the smell of spice and the noise of a restaurant bursting with life and happy, animated people. Aktor got up from the table shouting, 'Mr. Jones, Mr. Jones! I'm so pleased you've made it. Come and meet my mother! She's heard so much about you.'

Mr. Jones drank half a lager and felt acid swirling around his stomach. He made his excuse to leave before eating anything: 'I need to go to the hospital.' Aktor looked surprised, but it was not uncommon for Mr. Jones to visit patients out of hours. Jasmine normally hated it when he did, but with Jasmine in rehab he could do what he pleased. He drove back, and at the crossroads he hesitated. He could turn left to the hospital, or right to go home. He couldn't work out what to do. He felt stabbing pains of loneliness, and so he made a left turn, being in the hospital environment was much easier for him than being alone with these raw feelings. As a surgeon he could put on a mask.

He picked up a message from Jasmine saying that she was really enjoying rehab and feeling the benefits already, and that she wanted to be a proper wife and mother to their children, and that being in rehab made her realise how important her family was to her. So, he was in much better spirits.

****

Charlotte was sitting up in bed when he strode in with a beaming smile on his face. She looked shocked to see him. Probably because he looked transformed, wearing Levis and a white, collarless shirt.

Mr. Jones looked her up and down. 'Are you eating properly?'

There were no other patients on the ward apart from her. He surveyed her array of Clarins cosmetics on the table next to her bed. He looked at her in her white t-shirt and cotton check pyjamas. She looked vulnerable and fragile. He launched into a burbling speech about the Clarins men's range.

Charlotte looked at him in bemusement.

'I should be at an Indian restaurant.'

Charlotte was tempted to ask why he wasn't there, but didn't. She was conscious of the fact that she was wearing no make-up and that five minutes before seeing him walk onto the ward she'd been snivelling into her pyjamas, and now had visible damp patches down the front of her t-shirt. She felt vaguely irritated by this good-looking surgeon in his casual clothes, busting in on her vortex of misery, crying in the breast surgery ward. He just looked so gorgeous and she felt so naff. Mr. Jones looked even better than he did in his work clothes.

'Would you like a tissue? I should be at an Indian restaurant.'

'You've already said that.'

She felt a pang of sadness knowing she'd probably never drink a beer or have an Indian meal ever again or have a normal life. In the background there were fireworks going off outside, which added to the poignancy.

'Could I sit on your bed? Why are you shaking?'

'Because I'm frightened.'

Mr. Jones was tempted to put his arm around her but resisted. She looked so lost. 'I'd better go. I shouldn't really be here. I'd like to give you a hug but maybe I shouldn't.'

Sitting close to her, he took her hand and held it. He had long tapered fingers and perfectly cut nails. Then a familiar, very loud, female voice could be heard accompanied by heels clicking down the linoleum floor. The next moment Natasha walked in and looked at Charlotte and Mr. Jones, as he sprang away from her and jumped up from the bed.

'I didn't know you two knew each other,' said Mr. Jones. 'I'd better be going.' He exited the ward in two strides. Without looking back.

'Natasha, I didn't know you were coming.'

'Clearly,' replied Natasha. 'It all looked very cosy from where I was standing.'

'Oh, it's nothing, he's just being kind and doing his rounds. What are you all dressed up for?'

'I've just been out for drinks with my boys from the gym.'

'You mean your 20-somethings?'

'Why isn't Sam here?'

'He's at home, babysitting. His mum was supposed to babysit so he could visit me, but she's got a new illness this week. She's been reading her A–Z of symptoms again.'

'She's not got to H yet.'

'Hypochondria.' They both laughed.

'What do you think of Mr. Jones, then?'

'You mean Mr. Jones?'

'Is he fit? I was going to run off with my knee surgeon – but seriously Charlotte, what do you really think of him?'

'I'm really worried about him. I think he's going to get shot.'

'Shot?' replied Natasha. 'I think the anaesthetic or all the drugs they've given you are having an effect.'

'No. He's going to Afghanistan. I overheard someone saying so. He's going to train the local surgeons who are risking their lives and being paid a pittance. A lot of the surgeons there are taken up with limb amputations.'

Bridget Mary Woods came bustling in.

Natasha said to her, 'Charlotte's worried about Mr. Jones getting shot.'

'I overheard him talking to his colleague,' said Charlotte.

'Oh, he's more likely to get killed driving his car too fast here than getting shot in Afghanistan,' said Bridget, as she straightened Charlotte's bedding. 'We've been raising funds for the clinic out there.'

****

Mr. Jones was really excited about going to Afghanistan. His excitement made him overlook the actual danger of going there. He had felt really lonely with Jasmine away and wanted something to focus on. He loved surgery, with its highs and lows. It made him feel so alive that he could not only save someone's life but also make them look better, especially when that patient was someone like Charlotte – the all-adoring Charlotte. He felt a real man and loved the challenge. Even if post-surgery he was exhausted and spent when the adrenaline had ran out and he was back home alone.

Jasmine was surprisingly good about it when Dick told her he was going. In the past she had begged him not to go on any work-related trips, saying that he had responsibilities to her and their children, but he'd gone anyway. This time, surprisingly, she was agreeable when he told her. Perhaps now she finally understood his need for adventure and doing something humanitarian, whereas before she would say you can save lives here, you don't need to go off to a warzone to save lives.

Mr. Jones was to work alongside the Red Cross surgical team. His PhD was in wound healing, and he was to train in Afghanistan's most important hospitals, assisting the medical staff and helping them with more advanced techniques. His real motives for being there were, however, deeply hidden in the recesses of his mind, and he wasn't prepared to discover them just yet. He was simply aligned with the image of himself as the heroic surgeon going out to help the wounded.

15: Natasha

Fortunately for her, Natasha hadn't sustained any serious injuries from her fall at the gym – a cut to the head, bruising to one of her hips, nothing permanent. The worst thing was that she wasn't allowed to work out for two weeks. Mike - her husband - had told the reception staff at the gym not to let her in. She felt like a caged lion, restless and discontented. The lack of exercise meant an all-time endorphin low was hitting her bloodstream. She craved the gym like a junkie craves heroin. She needed a sweaty lycra fix.

Her overarching irritation and disappointment with Mike were escalating into World War Three. Sensing her disillusionment, Mike's *modus operandi* was to be extra thoughtful and jolly, buying her flowers and leaving little *I love you* notes under magnets on the fridge freezer. He kept offering to babysit the twins so she could have a night out with the girls. Natasha eventually agreed, as the gym crowd had invited her to a party.

That evening she pulled on a fitted pale pink lace top and a pair of ripped skinny jeans with tan suede wedges. She surveyed herself in the full-length mirror – she was gaining weight rapidly. She could already see it forming like spreadable Lurpak round her hips and bum. She was disgusted. She would have to go back to the gym. What if Luke saw her like this? Fortunately, he was in London on business, she had elicited from Augusta. But when she went out, she was still going to go by a different route to avoid going past his house, just in case. Normally she made a point of strolling past when she knew he was in residence.

The party turned out not to be the night Natasha had fantasised, it seemed like her 20-something boys all had 20-something girls on their arms. She thought she would go and commiserate with Sam instead, cheering him up. She power-walked – as much as you could in high wedges – 20 or so minutes from the party, via an off-licence, to Charlotte's house, and rang the doorbell.

It took a few minutes, but eventually Sam came to the door. He opened it just a crack. The door was on the chain and his eyes were red and puffy. He looked gaunt and stooped.

'The children are asleep,' he said to Natasha, discouragingly.

'I saw Charlotte in hospital earlier. I thought you might need some cheering up. You look like you could use a drink.'

She waved the bottle of Prosecco she'd purchased en route in Sam's face and he slowly undid the chain. She pushed the door further open and went in. Sam, his face visibly screwed up, went down the dimly lit hallway into the kitchen to find a couple of wine glasses.

'Oh fuck!' shouted Natasha, she caught her high heel on Felix's train that lay in the centre of the dark wooden floor as Charlotte wasn't around to tidy the toys up.

'Are you okay?'

'Yeah, I'm fine. I'm gonna need a fag now, though. Shall we go in the garden?'

'Oh, okay,' replied Sam.

Standing on the wet grass looking up at the sky, Natasha inhaled deeply, as though her life depended upon it.

'Can I have a cigarette?' asked Sam.

'You don't smoke,' replied Natasha, offering him the open packet.

Sam took one - Natasha lit it for him- 'Charlotte will have told you – she's having her lymph nodes removed to help stop the cancer spreading,' he said.

'You poor boy,' replied Natasha, stamping out her cigarette to give Sam a big bear hug. She squeezed him really tightly and for a few minutes they were suspended, locked in each other's arms.

Sam, suddenly feeling conscious that he might burn a hole in her jacket, unwrapped his arms from Natasha's slim body. 'Let's go back inside, the kids might wake up,' he said, stamping his cigarette out on the grass to avoid the decking.

Back inside he scrabbled around for matches, then lit the fire using Natasha's lighter. They sat on the chesterfield in the lounge, as one bottle of wine followed another, and then another.

'Shall we open another one?' Natasha suggested. She edged closer to Sam.

'I'm terrified she's going to die and I'm going to have to bring up the kids on my own. I can't say this to her.'

'Of course not. I mean no, of course she's not going to die. You've just hit a rough patch. So many women get breast cancer and recover.'

'I feel I need to reassure her, but I don't feel it myself. Or at least till we have the lymph node result.'

'She'll be fine, you just have to trust. The prognosis for breast cancer is so good these days.'

'I didn't realise how much I took her for granted till this happened. It really helps talking to you. I guess I haven't really admitted to myself, let alone anyone else, how frightened I am. I feel I have to be the tough guy.' He started crying, Natasha took his hand.

'You *are* a tough guy, you're gorgeous. Everyone's jealous of Charlotte.'

'Really?'

'Really.' Natasha dabbed his wet face with a tissue. 'I know what you need,' she said, reaching for her large - over-stuffed - handbag and pulling a joint from one of the many pockets. She lit it and passed it to Sam, who took a drag, started coughing, when he'd stopped - he continued to toke on it.

'Hey, let me have some!' she remonstrated. 'Have you never smoked a joint before?'

'No – I work in IT.'

She put her head on his shoulder, running her hand up his thigh, giving him a semi, she undid his jeans, dropped to her knees and started sucking on his cock - he groaned - he tried to pull away, but Natasha just pulled his hips forcefully with both arms - so that he came.

'Natasha, what are we doing? This isn't right and you know it's not right. You need to go.'

'Oh, I'm so sorry, I've had too much to drink. I was just so upset seeing Charlotte. Actually, I think I should warn you. Charlotte was with the surgeon *tête a tête*. I think I interrupted something.'

'What are you talking about? She's just had surgery. It's Saturday night.'

'Oh, I think I've got the wrong end of the stick. Forget I mentioned it.'

'I'm calling you a cab.'

'Don't worry, I can walk.'

Natasha grabbed her jacket and staggered out of the house, slamming the door behind her so that the whole house vibrated - prompting Felix to start wailing upstairs.

Thoughts...

Smoking
A Mum friend, who smoked post chemo, if I bumped into her having a fag. I would say "Do you know that smoking gives you cancer?" and we would both laugh.

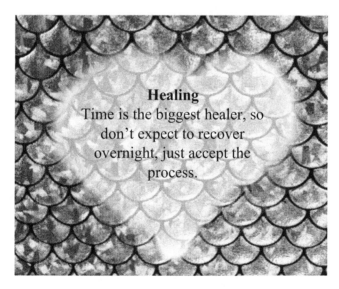

Healing
Time is the biggest healer, so don't expect to recover overnight, just accept the process.

16: Charlotte

Back at the hospital, the nurse called, 'Charlotte James', I got up out of my seat and walked towards the examination room, seeing Mr. Jones and Aktor in the room next door as I went in. My hands were trembling as I started to pull on the hospital gown for the post-operative examination. I could hear Mr. Jones's deep voice through the thin wall.

'How's Charlotte James? You saw her for her last appointment when I was at the conference.'

'She was disappointed not to see you and asked to know your whereabouts. I think she's got a bad case of FFS.'

'Really?'

'It could be terminal.''

I strained to hear more. FFS, what did that mean 'for fuck's sake'! It must be some form of cancer that they hadn't told me about, and I really *was* going to die. I legged it out of the examination room with my gown half-on half-off and my bum hanging out in an attempt to find Nurse Tough Love. Fortunately, she was just at the end of the corridor.

'Christ Charlotte, what's up?'

'I've got to talk to you,' I said with tears rolling down my face. 'I've got FFS.'

'I think we'd better go into a side room to have a chat.'

'I overheard Mr. Jones and Aktor talking about me.'

BMW started smiling.

'Why are you smiling?' I asked. 'This is serious.'

'Do you know what FfS stands for?'

'No of course I fucking don't.'

'It's Fallen for Surgeon.'

'Oh.'

'Yes,' said BMW. 'Just like NfC is Normal for Cornwall. And NoB is abbreviation for Night on Beer. Look, you're not the first and you won't be the last. You'd better go back into the examination room, but do up your hospital gown otherwise they'll wonder what's going on.'

Thoughts...

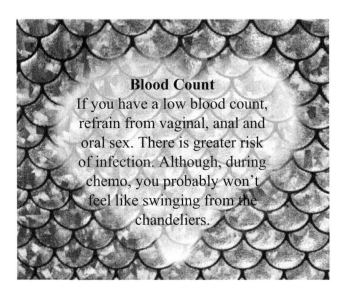

Blood Count
If you have a low blood count, refrain from vaginal, anal and oral sex. There is greater risk of infection. Although, during chemo, you probably won't feel like swinging from the chandeliers.

Pink
Not everyone with breast cancer wants to don pink lycra and run marathons. Resist the virtue signalling. Just do what is right for *you* and you alone.

17: Mr. Jones

Mr. Jones picked up his Dictaphone to compose Charlotte's letter to her GP, as he'd done for patients thousands of times. He paused for thought. What was it about her that he kept popping back to in his mind? Jasmine had now been in rehab for just over a month, and Mr. Jones visited her every two weeks. They would meet for a coffee, for just an hour on a Sunday. Jasmine seemed to be getting on okay. Mr. Jones refused to have couples counselling with her, as he saw it as her problem. She was the drinker, not him. He pressed Record.

'I saw Charlotte in the clinic today'

He was reminded of being taken to confession in church when he was little, before his mum had died. 'Bless me, Father, for I have sinned. It's been several weeks since my last confession. I keep thinking about another woman and I'm married. The thing is I love my wife, I've always loved my wife, so why am I thinking about Charlotte again? I think about her over breakfast and when I go to bed. I don't currently desire my wife. I know that's a terrible thing to say. I love her but I don't desire her. It's the drinking. By the time she went into rehab, she would only have sex with me when she was drunk. But just the smell of alcohol on her breath is now a complete turn-off for me, because she wanted the drink more than she wanted me. I know I shouldn't be thinking about Charlotte, because she's a patient, but I just have some sort of connection with her. Although she's not beautiful in the way that Jasmine is, I feel like I know her on a soul level. It's like a kindred spirit, she just seems to get what I'm talking about. I can talk to her for hours beyond medicine and cancer, whereas Jasmine loses concentration, and starts twitching for a drink. She doesn't seem to be there anymore, and Charlotte really is there. Why is this happening? I've never had feelings like this for a patient. I've always been professional but now I'm unravelling.'

He pressed delete and the confession was complete and erased. He started again: 'I saw an intelligent 43-year-old woman in the clinic today ...'

Mr. Jones had barely finished dictating before his phone rang and Jane said, 'You've got a Natasha Blake at reception here insisting on seeing you.'

He let out a sigh. 'Oh no, not her ...'

Thoughts...

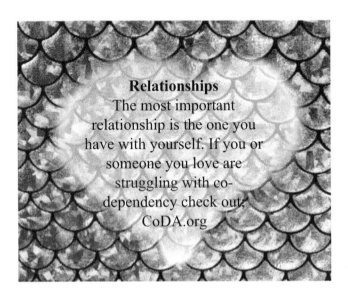

Relationships
The most important relationship is the one you have with yourself. If you or someone you love are struggling with co-dependency check out: CoDA.org

Cross Addiction
If you're struggling with cross addiction (giving up one substance for another) check out: panfellowship.org

18: Damien

Charlotte's ex Damien decided to put himself in rehab. Unbeknown to Charlotte, he had heard about her having breast cancer via the grapevine, so he had decided to stop drinking. At 9:30am on a Monday morning, he walked into the group therapy room. There was a circle of green plastic chairs, some occupied. He spotted a very slim, attractive blonde 40-year-old woman sitting with her legs crossed and sat down opposite her.

The walls of the room were painted light green, which was supposed to enhance the therapeutic atmosphere, but was doing little to lessen Damien's agitation. He hadn't drunk for three days and was desperate for a cigarette, but you were only allowed to smoke in the grounds. He had to make do with copious cups of strong coffee. The room was now full up and a counsellor came in to start the facilitation – The posh blonde woman was asked to speak first.

'My name's Jasmine,' she said in her cut-glass accent. 'I'm here because I can't stop drinking, and my husband thinks it's a good idea to be here.'

They then introduced themselves, going round in a circle clockwise until it got to Damien. When it was his turn he said, 'Hello, my name's Damien. I *suppose* you could say I'm an alcoholic.'

'*Are* you an alcoholic? Because if you ain't, you shouldn't be here,' said John, the counsellor, in his Mancunian drawl.

'Okay, I'm an alcoholic. I'm here because the woman I love has got breast cancer, it's made me realise how important she is to me. I don't want her to die. I want to be able to help and support her. It's made me realise what's important in life.'

'I'm not here for your sob stories, or for you to tell me how hard it is to quit drinking. I was in Broadmoor so I know the meaning of "hard",' said John.

The next two hours were spent in group therapy, with people telling their personal stories in lurid detail. John listened to each person but commented very little. He'd heard it all before. At 11 o'clock they broke for coffee. Damien followed Jasmine out into the garden. They both sat on a wooden bench - which had a plaque on it inscribed with the name of a former inmate who 'went back out there' in AA-speak. Jasmine just wanted some fresh air, but Damien was gasping for a fag.

'I don't smoke' said Jasmine when he offered her a cigarette.

He lit up. 'Are you sure?' he said, taking another drag.

'Oh, okay,' said Jasmine, taking it from him, inhaling, then blowing smoke in his direction. She laughed as he tried to swat the smoke away from his face, and then he started laughing too.

'So how did you end up here?' enquired Jasmine.

'It was my partner's fault - Stacey – she's a drinker. When I met her, I had every intention of quitting and going to rehab, but it's very difficult to stop drinking when somebody's drinking loads around you. I wanted to marry Charlotte, but she gave me an ultimatum – it was either her or the drink. Meanwhile, Stacey was waving a bottle of drink and I couldn't resist. Now I realise she was only interested in my brother.'

'Your brother?'

'Yeah' said Damien. 'He's Jack Rashleigh, The Rash.'

'Oh my god,' said Jasmine. 'That's seriously impressive.'

Jasmine and Damien were late back to that afternoon session. 'Where the fuck have you two been?' barked John.

Thoughts...

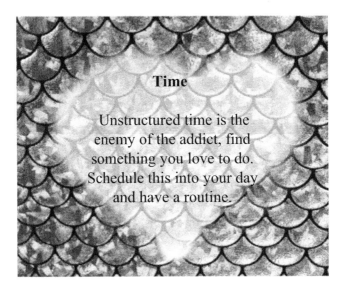

Time

Unstructured time is the enemy of the addict, find something you love to do. Schedule this into your day and have a routine.

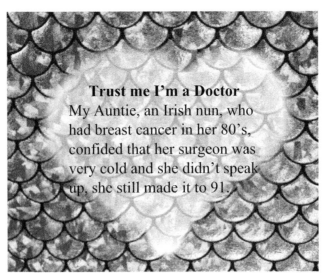

Trust me I'm a Doctor
My Auntie, an Irish nun, who had breast cancer in her 80's, confided that her surgeon was very cold and she didn't speak up, she still made it to 91.

19: Charlotte

As much as I'd been desperate to leave the hospital, trying to recover from surgery back at home with two small children - was not an easy thing. Sam didn't have a clue how to cook a meal, so I was doing stupid things like bending down over a hot oven, I was determined that as a family, we would still eat substantially well. I also wanted to keep physically fit and did all the prescribed exercises to avoid any weakness or stiffness, which truly exhausted me.

One day I was standing up, with my weight against the wall, doing press-ups to build up my upper body strength again, on the 'Use it or lose it' basis. Suddenly, I felt the most excruciating pain in my left breast, the one which had been reconstructed. I screamed for Sam. He was in the other room and came rushing into the bedroom.

'What's going on?' he said.

I fell to the floor clutching my chest. My boob was getting bigger and bigger and as I ripped my top off, I could see the straining at the stitches.

'Call an ambulance!' I screamed at Sam.

Even though I was in my excruciating pain, it felt like a bomb was going off in my chest. I could see the comedic side of things and thought of all those tacky magazines with horror stories like, *My Boob Exploded!* Sam rang the hospital, because we couldn't understand what was happening. I was screaming with agony. Minutes later, Jim the paramedic walked in. I've never been so happy to see him in my life. He's Josh's dad from school and was hugely strapping, which is what you want when you're doubled up and need to be carried out. In the ambulance he asked me what had happened, and I pulled my top up to show him.

I kept saying 'It's breast cancer, it's breast cancer. Even in my agonised state I didn't want him to think I'd had a boob job, even though it was really obvious: you wouldn't have just one boob done and save up for the other one. Jim quickly administered morphine to my arm, which instantly took the pain away. I held his hand all the way to the hospital. I felt such relief that the pain had gone. The siren in the ambulance behind was really loud. I couldn't understand why it was so loud, why didn't it just overtake us? Unbeknown to me, it was the siren of the ambulance I was actually in, and it was Sam's car behind. Months later the kids would still tease me about Paramedic Jim, saying 'Why did you go all funny around Josh's dad?' I'd laugh and say it was just the memory of the morphine. It's so amazing when you're in so much pain. Felix would giggle and say Josh's dad gave Mummy the kiss of life.

On arrival at the hospital, I was greeted by Nurse Tough Love, who had a smile on her face. I was supposed to be having Welcome to Chemo today. 'I'm wondering if you're using this as an excuse to get out of chemo, or it's just an excuse to see Mr. Jones again.' She asked.

The pain had subsided, so I laughed along with her.

Then Mr. Jones walked in the door. I was lying on the couch *en déshabille*. 'What's up with you, Trouble?' he said. Which made me laugh, as that was Jack Rashleigh's nickname for Damien. Mr. Jones examined me, and said 'You need an urgent operation. You have a haematoma, a bleed, so I'll have to take the implant out and redo it.'

I found myself back on the ward again, this time with no overnight bag, no toothbrush, no mobile phone charger. Sam had to go and get the kids from school. How could this have happened? After completing his ward round, Mr. Jones came back and visited me.

'I've managed to get a slot tomorrow to do the surgery,' he said. He glanced down - or at least I thought he glanced down - at the cosmetics bag on my bed. I felt embarrassed. Another patient had lent it to me as I didn't have anything with me, but the washbag was frilly and chavvy and garish, and even though it was a life-or-death experience, I wanted to shout 'This isn't my wash bag!'. I couldn't believe how vacuous I was to care about something so trivial, and he probably hadn't even clocked it anyway. Mr. Jones followed my gaze, picked up the pink frilly washbag and said; 'My 10-year-old daughter would wrestle you to the ground for this.'

We both laughed. I then felt really ungrateful to the kind lady who'd given it to me, but I shoved it in the cabinet next to my bed nonetheless.

Thoughts...

Life

Cancer doesn't have to rule your life, find a new project or something, or someone to distract yourself.

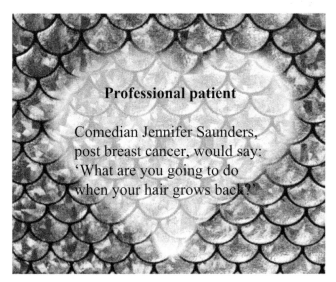

Professional patient

Comedian Jennifer Saunders, post breast cancer, would say: 'What are you going to do when your hair grows back?'

20: Damien

It was mid-morning break, and in the gardens of the treatment center, nestled in the countryside, it had just started to rain. Damien and Jasmine had taken cover, underneath a beech tree whose large branches fanned out like an umbrella, keeping them dry. Damien was having a cigarette, but Jasmine just wanted fresh air. The two of them had buddied up, and Jasmine was enthralled by Damien's stories of growing up with Jack Rashleigh as his younger brother, which he had shared in the group. Jasmine normally abhorred smoking, but these intimate moments with Damien after the emotional turmoil of group therapy meant that she was now having the odd puff of Damien's cigarette.

She was normally far too vain about ageing her skin, or her clothes smelling of smoke, to even think about something so unattractive in her eyes. Even Dick had commented on the smell of smoke when he made a brief visit one weekend and hugged her on arrival. Jasmine denied it, saying 'Everyone's smoking here because they're not drinking, and it's wafting over me. I can't stand it either.' Until recently in most AA meetings, you couldn't even see the faces of most people, because of the veil of cigarette smoke.

Damien was also incredibly funny and had Jasmine in girlish stitches, in and out of group. 'Tell me about Mr. Jones then,' said Damien. 'Is he a Mr. Jones or is he the great surgeon?'

'He's a saint, but he's very much knife before wife,' replied Jasmine.

'He put his patients before you? You're the sinner, then. The demon drinker,' said Damien.

'Did you say you have a girlfriend? Or was alcohol your mistress?'

'Yes and no.'

'What does that mean?'

'I don't love the one I'm with. I love someone else.'

'So, explain.'

'I love Charlotte, but I'm with Stacey.'

'Why is that?'

'I was with Charlotte for five years, and she dumped me because of my drinking. I really messed up with her. Now she's married with kids.'

'Do you have any kids?'

'Yeah, but he's grown up and lives in Sydney with his mother.'

'Do you want any more?'

'No, I've had the snip.'

'So, are Charlotte and Stacey alike?'

'No, they're opposites. Charlotte's intelligent, tall and dark. Stacey's a local girl, brassy, blonde and short, but she's impressed by the celebrity world and believes my bullshit. Charlotte isn't. Charlotte wouldn't have me, unless I stopped drinking. Stacey's always waving a bottle of wine and offering sex. Who can resist? She also loves dressing up and wearing high heels. She's desperate for a baby and we're engaged. But Charlotte's the one I love and I want to get sober for her. Especially now she's got breast cancer.'

'Breast cancer? Oh god, she's not one of Mr. Jones patients, is she?'

'I don't know.'

'Why did you get engaged to Stacey?'

'To take it up a level.'

'You sound like Prince Charles.'

'Well, that didn't end well.'

'So does Stacey know about Charlotte?'

'She thinks we're not in touch any more. She's got a very jealous streak and she wouldn't tolerate that. But I'm sick of the drunken rows we have, and waking up feeling remorseful. Stacey would go crazy if she thought I was in touch with Charlotte. I don't want her leaving any more drunken messages on Charlotte's phone. She once left a message on New Year's Day for Charlotte, saying, "Enjoy your misery, he's coming back to you" in such an upbeat tone, she sounded almost happy. In truth, Charlotte doesn't want me back. She gave me an ultimatum: it was either the drink or her, and I chose the drink. I know I've been weak, and you?'

'Well, I could never measure up to Mr. Jones. Everyone thinks he's wonderful. He's so adored and admired. All his patients are in love with him. It makes me sick. He's Mr. Goody-Two-Shoes,' Jasmine said.

'He sounds like my brother. We're both black sheep then. Jack always says to me, "Why don't you just have *one*?"'

'The thing is, we *can't* just have one, can we?' said Jasmine, and started giggling. 'Is Jack bankrolling you?'

'Yes,' said Damien.

'I drink because I can't ever live up to Mr. Jones, I'm not very well cast as the great surgeon's wife. I have no place, no identity next to the great man. He's always at work, and quite frankly I'm bored, that's why I hang out in Knightsbridge and shop and end up having a liquid lunch – I don't eat anything, I just pick at a couple of olives and drink champagne on my own. That's the only excitement I have in my life.'

'You need to come with me to LA and meet Jack.'

'Well, I will, when I get out of this place. That's the incentive then, for us to get out of here.'

Thoughts...

Breathing
Set an alarm on your phone to remind yourself to *breathe*. It is very easy to drown in the day-to-day dramas. Breathe in for four counts and out for eight.

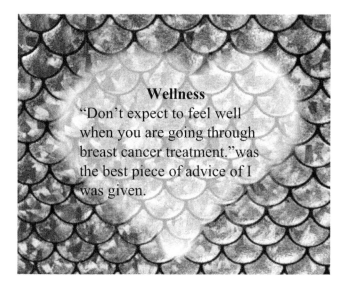

Wellness
"Don't expect to feel well when you are going through breast cancer treatment."was the best piece of advice of I was given.

21: Natasha

Natasha was sitting in the waiting room - flicking through gossip magazines to kill time. She was Mr. Jones's last patient, having been tacked on the end of his busy clinic. It was going to be a long wait, with all the other people there, but she figured it was worth it. Natasha, to her horror, suddenly spotted a picture of Luke entwined with a 20-something blonde, at some launch in London. It was like a stab through the heart. She felt physically sick. No wonder she hadn't heard from Luke for a while. If Luke was going to be unfaithful to Augusta, it had to be with *her* and not some 20-something. She was already feeling awful after her dalliance with Sam – but worse, that morning when she'd been in a health food shop, looking for some potion to make herself feel better, or at least younger. The sales assistant had called over to her, 'We've got special offers today for OAPs.' At 48, Natasha was horrified. She'd headed towards the Ladies, pulled out a cosmetics bag stashed with make-up, found her mirror - which she balanced precariously on the window ledge. She started applying several rounds of mascara, over the already existing blobs of eye make-up. The more foundation she put on her face the more her lines were visible, which wasn't helped by the harsh daylight pouring through the toilet window. She'd now achieved a clown effect, looking more ET than an attractive mature woman. She added the finishing touches of red lipstick.

Natasha had that familiar feeling: jealousy of other women. She even felt competitive towards the other women in the waiting room, vying for Mr. Jones's time and attention. But it was her jealousy of Charlotte that was bubbling over. Why was it, she thought, that everyone wanted Charlotte? Sam, Damien and now even Mr. Jones. She'd spotted Charlotte with him on the ward.

Finally, Natasha was called in.

'Okay, Mrs. Blake, I've got your file here. I understand you've recently received the good news that, you don't carry the BRCA gene, so what can I do for you?' said Mr. Jones.

'I've found a lump and I need you to check it out.'

'You've found a lump.'

'Yes. I need you to examine me.'

'You need to go and see your GP and possibly have a mammogram.'

'But I'm so worried.' she said. 'Could you not just look at me now?'

Mr. Jones paused. He noticed her figure-hugging, wraparound dress.

'Okay, if you want to just get changed behind the curtain.'

A few minutes later, Natasha presented herself. She was wearing matching see-through Agent Provocateur worn once underwear that she'd found off eBay.

'Do you want to put a gown on?'

Mr. Jones examined her in a very cold, medical way, lacking any possible vibe. 'So, where's the lump?'

Natasha guided his hand to her breast.

'I can't feel anything,' he said palpating her right breast.

'Well, it was there this morning. I felt it in the shower.'

He felt the area of flesh again. 'There's no lump.'

'Couldn't it be a breast mouse?'

'No, it's not a fibroadenoma. They're mobile but easily spotted. You don't have one of those. Do you want to get dressed and we will have a chat?'

Natasha pulled on her clothes. When she was fully dressed he said: 'So, where do we go from here?'

'Where would you like to go from here?' said Natasha raising her eyebrows.

'I suggest making a referral, via your GP, for some counselling. I think that the shock of the BRCA gene scare has disturbed you, and you might need some extra support.'

Natasha was furious and stormed out. She was so angry that she forgot her mobile phone, which was normally glued to her ear. She did a U-turn and headed back to the examination room. She was just about to push open the door when she heard Mr. Jones's voice: 'I met with this 48-year-old ageing nympho today, who insisted on an appointment at my busy clinic, which is for women who have a life-threatening condition.'

Natasha pushed the door open. Mr. Jones pressed delete. Natasha grabbed her phone from the couch without saying a word to him. He pressed a button on his answer machine and heard Jane's tones: 'Apologies, but I've had to leave on time today. If you could put Natasha Blake's file back that would be great.'

Natasha went back into the waiting room where she sat down and texted Augusta: 'Have you seen that compromising picture of Luke?' Then she texted Charlotte, her husband Mike and other close friends. 'I've got breast cancer too.'

Natasha went to the only place she could think of to get relief, the gym, and did the most strenuous work-out of her life. Even the young 20-somethings at the gym were amazed at her strength and determination.

****

It was a spring morning and Dick was driving to work. He was in a good mood and had a smile on his face. Things were improving with Jasmine. She'd been doing so well, there was talk of her going to a Halfway House in South Kensington, to start the second phase of her recovery. She also seemed a lot happier in herself. He was also excited about seeing Charlotte again in his clinic. His mobile rang and he switched it on to loudspeaker. It was Aktor, sounding worried.

'Natasha Blake's dead.'

Dick replied, 'I'll be there in 10 minutes.'

'Sir Hugh's demanding to see you straight away.'

Despite the waiting room full to the brim, Dick was summoned in to see Sir Hugh.

'Come in and sit down, Dick, we're in deep shit. Your patient Natasha Blake's dead. The family have threatened to sue us. Could you please explain to me why you allowed a patient in obvious distress at being diagnosed with breast cancer, to leave the hospital unaccompanied and without being offered any support or counselling?'

'What happened to her?'

'Cardiac arrest. Her family are calling for your head. We haven't been able to locate her file. What's going on, Dick?'

'She's not got breast cancer and I referred her for counselling. This is a witch hunt.'

Thoughts...

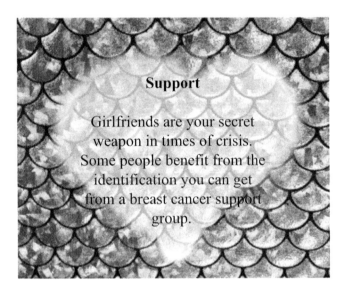

Support

Girlfriends are your secret weapon in times of crisis. Some people benefit from the identification you can get from a breast cancer support group.

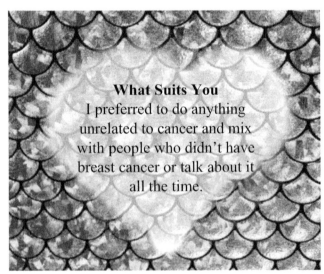

What Suits You
I preferred to do anything unrelated to cancer and mix with people who didn't have breast cancer or talk about it all the time.

22: Charlotte

It was the night before Natasha's funeral. I was in shock. Physical shock from being discharged from the hospital, having had my implant replaced two days earlier, and mental shock from hearing the news about Natasha. I sat at the kitchen table, my body curling in on itself, my shoulders hanging off my ears like giant earrings. The children were unusually asleep. Sam was clearing dishes and loading the dishwasher as tears trickled down my face.

'I need a hug,' I said to Sam.

'Let me finish loading the dishwasher first,' he replied.

'I'd thought I was the one that was going to die, not Natasha. Why has this happened? She's my best friend. She's so full of life, well was. Always up to something. She's such a loyal friend,' I wailed.

Sam continued loading the dishes, making louder crashing noises as he did so.

'She was such a good friend to me. I don't know what I'm going to do without her. She was supposed to get me through this. Not die.'

'She wasn't that good a friend,' said Sam angrily.

'What do you mean? That's a really horrible thing to say.'

'Well, when you were in hospital, she came round here.'

'Yeah, I know she did.'

'She'd been drinking and she made a pass at me.'

'Why are you telling me this now? Why don't you just keep that to yourself?'

'Because I don't want you to be misled.'

'I hope you didn't respond.'

'I tried not to.'

'Tried not to? I was in hospital having treatment for cancer, and you say you tried not to. What does that mean?'

'Well, what about you and Mr. Jones?'

'I can't believe what I'm hearing.' I left the room. I threw myself on the bed, clutching my chest protectively. I couldn't believe Sam would do this. I couldn't believe that Natasha would do this. I couldn't believe that Sam would tell me this, on the eve of her funeral. Those poor boys have been left without a mother. I didn't even want to go to the funeral now. I didn't know what to believe.

****

It was pouring with rain when we turned up at the village church, where Mike and Natasha had got married. That had been such a happy day. Today there was a huge turn-out. It was agony seeing the grey faces of Natasha's twin boys, Samson and Charlie, and Mike, looking as if the light had gone out of their lives. For all of Mike's plodding ways, he'd adored Natasha. He always forgave her for her dalliances. The boys looked really smart in matching little ties and jackets. Augusta and Luke were in the second row, Augusta in an *haute couture* black silk suit.

I had rehearsed this scene so many times in my head, but for my funeral, not Natasha's. I couldn't believe she was in this box, covered in wreaths of lilies, her and my favourite flowers. The coffin looked so small. I guess, she didn't have to worry about her weight now. We'd always joked about how we'd be thin when we were dead. The scent of lilies and beeswax candles wafted around the church, there was a large plasma screen to the side of the pulpit for those at the back.

Just before the service was about to begin, I noticed a familiar face appearing at the back. 'There's your surgeon guy,' Sam whispered in my ear. God, I wonder why he's here, I thought to myself. He doesn't even know her. She wasn't even his patient.

The vicar did a fairly good eulogy, bearing in mind Natasha didn't spend much time in church apart from at weddings and very merry at Christmas. The last song was Tasha's favourite, we exited our pew to Abba's 'Dancing Queen' – I remember dancing to this so many times with her. Everyone started clapping and I swivelled round to see, the big screen lit up with Tasha and me dancing to Abba's hit. We were laughing, and Tasha was blowing kisses. Her boys started dancing camply down the aisle. It was her finale.

Sam grabbed my hand, which was odd, as he's not really into public displays of affection. I looked down at the floor as we passed Mr. Jones in a grey tailored suit, standing alone in a pew.

The rain had stopped and Sam disappeared off to find the car to go to the wake. Mr. Jones was standing away from all the friends and relatives. I felt uncomfortable about blanking him in the church and as Sam was getting the car, I went up to him. He was shifting his weight from one leg to the other, looking at his watch repeatedly. I felt relieved when he looked up and smiled.

'Good dancing.'

I blushed. 'I didn't expect to see you here.'

'Shouldn't you be resting? I was really sorry to hear about Natasha. She's not my patient, but the hospital thought in view of what happened, it would be a good idea for me to attend.'

'Why wasn't she your patient, if she'd got breast cancer?'

'She hadn't got breast cancer.'

'Oh. The last message I got from her said she had it.'

'I shouldn't be discussing a patient, but she didn't have breast cancer. She died following a cardiac arrest due to exertion. I've said too much already.'

Then he leaned forward and kissed me on the cheek. He smelt of fresh laundry and testosterone, which was intoxicating.

'I'm sorry about your friend,' he said and turned to go.

I gazed at Mr. Jones as he strode towards the car park. His height was impressive. Just then Sam appeared. The two men passed each other without exchanging a word, or eye contact. My phone beeped. It was a text from Damien: 'I can't believe the news about Tasha. Sorry I couldn't make the funeral. I'm in LA. Marry me?'

I thought back to the first time that Damien had proposed. It was the early days and we were on holiday in St Just on the Roseland, a peninsula overlooking the sea in Cornwall. It was a beautiful sunny day. He hugged me and got out a small gold band with diamonds embedded in it, and said: 'Marry me?' Of course, I replied 'Yes.' The church and the churchyard on the Roseland were stunning, and I wanted to get married there, as do hundreds of other DFLs.

We'd booked the local boutique hotel, mainly hosting would-be second-homers. We were to have the mosaic terrace, which looked out on to the sea. We'd taken Damien's mum for dinner there one sunny Sunday evening, which should have been idyllic given the venue and location, but it wasn't. We'd shared a bottle of champagne with the owner of the hotel, who was also a writer. I chatted to him about journalism, and I got all giggly from the champagne. Damien was furious and lambasted me when we got home, accusing me of flirting with the owner, and said something about my drinking.

But there was no 'my drinking'. I rarely drank more than two glasses. Especially if I was wearing heels. It was more a case of, 'his drinking'.

We had been going to charter the hotel's yacht around the bay, arriving at the wedding reception by boat. Instead of a formal sit-down dinner, we would have canapés and flutes of champagne, passed around by waiters on silver trays. Spending our honeymoon at Lake Garda.

Damien's mum, Molly, had been going to do a duet with me because of her experience as an actress and singer. This was quite intimidating in view of, the fact that Jack Rashleigh would be in the audience – he would probably start booing when he heard my singing. We were going to do a cheesy number, 'You're Just Too Good to Be True', by Frank Sinatra. Start singing the opening line, 'You're just too good to be true, I can't take my eyes off you,' and then Molly and I were going to hoik up our dresses to the refrain, 'I love you, baby, and it's quite all right, I need you baby, to warm the lonely nights, I love you baby, trust in me when I say ...' It was going to be a surprise for Damien.

But Damien's drinking had put paid to all that. The reality, if we had got married, it would have been Damien getting drunk the night before the wedding, and picking on me till I cracked. Me crying all night, and waking up looking puffy-eyed and ugly the next morning. Not being able to face any wedding, let alone mine.

I do recall there was another proposal, on Boxing Day, the Christmas we split up. I'd booked myself into a Buddhist retreat for the entire Christmas period to get over the break-up. It was a silent retreat, and I was horrified to find that on Christmas Eve, there wasn't going to be anything for dinner, being Buddhist, we were to remember the less fortunate. I had a hacking cough and a chest infection to match. I really needed feeding, so went into the kitchen, all tear-stained, and managed to get a piece of bread and a bit of cheese to get me through.

I'd had a session that afternoon with Ken, a former soldier turned Buddhist monk, from Manchester. He'd roared with laughter when I told him my story. 'You're never going to get your needs met by an alcoholic.'

Then on Boxing Day I'd got Damien's marriage proposal text. I'd just ignored it, knowing what the monk had said was true, even though I didn't like it.

****

Now, at the church, Sam said, 'Hurry up, get in the car.'

'What's the rush?' I replied, watching Mr. Jones on his phone in the distance, pacing the car park.

Thoughts...

Feel Good
Get measured properly and get yourself matching sexy underwear. The lady who fitted me for a raspberry satin bra said "That's the best reconstruction I have ever seen."

Confidence

Do not compare and despair.

23: Stacey

It was 10 o'clock in the morning, Stacey was scrutinising her face in the mirror. She was pushing 40, and a lifetime of drink, cigarette smoking and late nights was showing on her skin. Dark roots were emerging beneath her bleached blonde hair. She opened the bathroom cabinet in search of some concealer, and out fell four pregnancy kits. She was desperate for a baby but Damien wouldn't get himself checked out. He'd said he'd already fathered a child, so the problem must be hers, but she'd been checked out and everything seemed to be fine. She hadn't seen Damien for a few weeks as he'd been in LA with Jack. The last thing he'd said to her before he left was, 'I'm going to come back with an agent and my own TV show.'

Stacey's mobile sprang into life. It was Damien. 'How are you doing, babe?' he asked.

'Good,' she said. 'When are you coming home? I'm really missing you.'

'Well, things are going really well here. I've been in a lot of meetings with Jack and production companies. So, it looks like things are in the bag. How's things with you babe?'

'I've been asked to do an interview and glamour shoot.'

'What do you mean, a glamour shoot?'

'They've asked me to talk about my boob job.'

'Who are they?'

'The *Daily News*.'

'How much did they offer you?

'£500 for the interview, and £500 for pictures.'

Stacey heard a woman's cutglass English accent in the background. 'Who's that?' she demanded.

'Oh, I'm going to have to go, It's Jack's new P.A. We've got a limo waiting outside. Tell them I'm handling the story and we want £2000.'

'Are you still working at the pub?'

'Yes, 16 hours so I can get working tax credits, why?'

'When the *Daily News* asks you how you paid for your boob job, say you saved up your benefits.'

'Ok, Love you.'

'Love you too.'

Stacey put the phone down. 'Why is he getting a limo at 2 o'clock in the morning?' she wondered aloud. It must be Jack keeping nocturnal hours.

Thoughts...

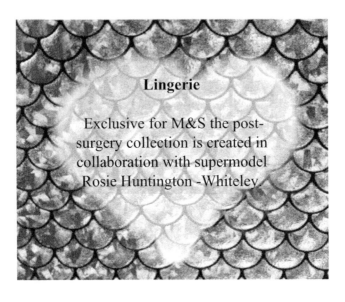

Lingerie

Exclusive for M&S the post-surgery collection is created in collaboration with supermodel Rosie Huntington -Whiteley.

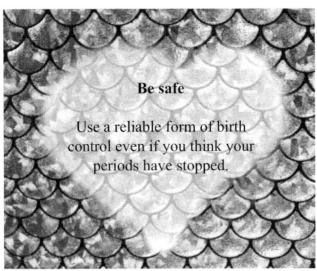

Be safe

Use a reliable form of birth control even if you think your periods have stopped.

24: Charlotte

The day I was dreading was finally here. I was going to lose my looks, and my health overnight. But, as I'd constantly been reminded by BMW, I would hopefully get to live at the end of it, and attend my daughter Sophie's wedding, albeit this wish was a bit premature.

Sam dropped me at the entrance to the clinic for my Welcome-to-Chemo session. The nurse who was running the session, and asking me various questions and keying my answers into a tablet, was hugely overweight. I did want to ask him if, I was going to get really fat during treatment. Some people really bloat and pile on weight when they do chemo, largely due to the steroids, I think. Although others get really thin. But I kept my question to myself. Any hypothetical weight gain on my part was unlikely to elicit much sympathy from the corpulent nurse.

I had spoken to BMW at length, mainly about losing my hair. In fact, any time there was a lull in conversation, I would pipe up with: 'Are you sure I'm going to lose my hair?' To which she would reply with a resounding 'Yes!'. I had also asked if I could wait till autumn/winter to do chemo, rather than in the height of summer when wearing a hat draws attention to yourself.

'The thing is,' said BMW, 'so many women focus on losing their hair, yet don't really consider losing a breast. After all, hair grows back.' Also, I didn't opt for the cold cap, which was supposed to help retain your hair. Freezing to death was not my thing, I am a sunworshipper.

After the Welcome-to-Chemo was over, I decided I needed some retail therapy, so I went shopping. I had a couple of hours to kill, before my clinical appointment with Mr. Jones. I walked into the first shoe shop that I saw and purchased some beige suede wedged-heel sandals. They looked great on in the shop, so I decided to wear them out and got the sales assistant to bin my flat worn-out pumps. But the streets of Truro are incredibly cobbly, and within five minutes of leaving the shop I nearly twisted my ankle. I had visions of me going into chemo in plaster and on crutches. Arriving on flat ground again at the hospital sometime later, I sauntered into the clinic with an hour to kill. I couldn't face any more shopping in *those* heels. I sat down and started reading a magazine.

Minutes later Mr. Jones appeared. Despite the heaving clinic and the fact that I was an hour early, he said: 'I can see you now. Follow me.' Gently closing the door of the examination room, and turning to me, his gaze focusing intently upon me, he said: 'You've just hit a rough patch. You'll get through this.'

BMW handed me a gown, and Mr. Jones examined my reconstructed breast and pronounced that it was healing properly.

'Nice shoes, by the way', said Mr. Jones. 'Shame you can't walk in them.' His expression turned into a grin as he gave me a hug, and left the room.

I burst into tears and BMW put her arms around me, as I nestled into her starchy uniform, trails of snot, resembling the Brooklyn Bridge started to form between me and her.

****

I was sitting in a candy-pink-plastic-high-backed chair. Other chemo patients alongside and in front of me, laid out in care home formation. We were all looking at each other and trying not to look. The chemo. nurse appeared by my side with various needles.

Natasha was supposed to be here to jolly me along. Why did she have to die at a time like this? Instead, Pauline had come, my lovely neighbour, who was a mother substitute. She was in her seventies and had five grown-up children, but had found the time to come and hold my hand.

The nurse applied a tourniquet to my arm and remarked: 'What beautiful veins you've got. They'll be so easy to cannulate.'

I just wanted to scream the place down and shout, 'I'm a health journalist. This can't be happening!' The needle went in, and the cold bleach shot into my body via my beautiful veins. It was not actually bleach, it was *Carboplatin* which sounds like car battery acid. Thank f**k it wasn't *FEC*, which was supposed to be, a particularly nasty chemo drug, at least according to the cancer grapevine.

The day went remarkably quickly, as I was chatting to my neighbour most of the time. The NHS provided plastic sandwiches and stewed tea for lunch - not a bloody Fortnum & Masons hamper in sight. There was also an absence of *Twinings'* ginger tea to help with the nausea.

The hardest part of the day was being stuck next to Bob. Radon-Bob was a lovely man in his late sixties who was having chemo for his asbestosis, having worked with asbestos all his life. His only failing was that he had one topic of conversation which was radon gas. It was like being stuck next to the bore at a dinner party. But aside from this, the bore was terrifying me.

He believed radon was responsible for all cancers, despite the lack of any scientific proof. Cornwall was a hotspot for radon gas release, due to all the granite. I disputed his theory as I've lived in London all my life and so it was highly unlikely that I'd have succumbed to radon gas poisoning, in the short time I'd lived here. Unfortunately though, this wasn't a dinner party, and as I was wired up to the drip stand, which was emitting its bleach, I couldn't get away from Radon-Bob and his theories. I tried to focus my mind on something else. Anything to distract me. I tried to give myself mental pain of a different flavour.

This is random, I felt guilty about the previous prime minister. I owed him an amend. The chubby nurse who had given me the introduction said that it was under the last government that the state-of-the-art chemo suite had been funded and could open. Previously it had been located in the dungeon of the hospital, a dreary and depressing place with no windows and dimly lit. More suitable for hangings than medical rebirth.

I thought back to my London days, in newspaper land. This wasn't my finest hour and I felt good old Catholic guilt about it. I heard in my head, the childhood refrain 'Forgive me Father, for I have sinned. It has been so many weeks since I have been to confession.' As I child I used to make up stuff I had done, for something to say. But not this time. Was I going to enter the gates of Hell, or be spared and enter Heaven? Or actually survive?

It had been quite a cold spring Monday morning back in 2003, when I found myself blinking in the sunlight outside 10 Downing Street, with my magazine editor. I was freelance. I remember feeling quite bored that morning, that restless discontent that usually spells trouble. I should have been excited. I had done a health commission and the prime minister and his wife were hosting a brunch reception for the people I had used as case studies. One was a group of nurses who wanted to give up smoking. Then there were four Afro-Caribbean sisters who were all morbidly obese, trying to lose weight. And the mum of a three-year-old who had Down's syndrome, who had no 'Me time'. I was to write about their struggle, with reducing their stress levels and improving their overall health.

The prime minister and his wife were very chatty and forthcoming. They seemed to have a real chemistry between them, which indicated a happy marriage. I'd told my editor that morning that according to the press, their young son had been rushed tó hospital over the weekend. She asked after him. When it was first reported in the Sunday newspapers, there had been no mention of why he'd been rushed to hospital. His mother said he'd come off his bike and possibly had concussion, so was being checked out to err on the side of safety. She knew we were both journalists but she did not say this was off the record.

When the reception had ended, I was back outside on the pavement again with my editor, she said, 'I was wondering what to do about the prime minister's son.' She wanted to use the story, but couldn't because her mag was a weekly. It was such a scoop. I didn't know what to do, so I rang Damien.

He picked up immediately, which was unusual for him on a Monday morning, at least after a heavy weekend.

'I've got a dilemma', I said, and gave him the details.

'Use it, use it, use it,' he urged me. 'Actually, if you don't use it, I will.'

'Okay,' I said. 'I'll call you later.'

I then rang the paper I normally freelanced for and gave them the scoop. They were delighted.

The next day I picked up a voicemail from my magazine editor: 'The *Daily News* has run a story about the prime minister's son. Is this anything to do with you? Because if it is, you're now banned from the magazine. And by the way, the Press Complaints Commission are on it.'

Oh god, why did I listen to Damien? It wasn't the right thing to do. He always got me into trouble.

Like all things in life, it seemed a big deal at the time. The prime minister and his wife were furious about having their privacy invaded. But then it was all forgotten about, when the Gulf War blew up a few weeks later and weapons of mass destruction entered the vernacular.

****

Sam came to pick me up, looking glum, after my first day of chemo. 'I need to get some petrol. The tank's nearly empty,' he said.

'Okay,' I said. I sat in the passenger seat staring into space. I noticed Sam pulling a face as he was putting petrol in the car.

'What's up?' I said after he'd paid and got back into the car.

'Squeezing the pump, it's really hurt my hand.' He rubbed it as he shifted in his seat.

'I'm not really the best person to say that to today,' I said as we pulled out of the forecourt back onto the main road.

Thoughts...

Kindness
Not all surgeons are alike. The relationship you have with your surgeon is important. A good bedside manner is not necessarily a given but a gift.

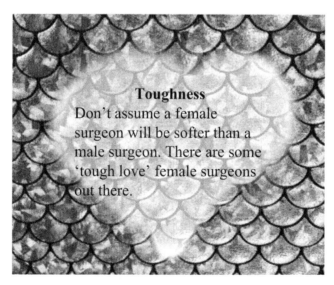

Toughness
Don't assume a female surgeon will be softer than a male surgeon. There are some 'tough love' female surgeons out there.

25: Mr. Jones

At 7 o'clock the next morning, Aktor was pacing the corridor of the hospital, clutching a copy of the *Daily News*. His eyes darted left to right as patients on the ward were beginning to wake up, the health care assistant with a trolley of stewed tea was starting her round. Earlier, he had seen the nurses at the nurse's station, looking at the tabloid and wondered what the fuss was about. He found Dick in the deserted patients lounge, with his head in his hands.

'There you are!' Aktor exclaimed. 'I'm going to make your day worse now'

'I've already seen it.' He replied.

'The prime minister has called for no more boob jobs on benefits. Wasn't she one of your private clients?' he said, thrusting the newspaper paper into Dick's lap. On the front cover was a picture of Stacey, her hands on her waist, sticking out her breasts, wearing a T-shirt two sizes too small, looking incredibly pleased with herself. The headline ran: '*No Boobs on Benefits.*'

'Regrettably, she was' Dick replied.

Dick had never owed a penny in his life. He had his Dad to thank for that but with Jasmine's excessive spending, the debts were piling up. The only way he could see out of it, was to take on private work. Which meant non-medical breast enlargements. By accepting more private work, he felt he was letting his mother down.

His phone rang, he picked up and uttered 'Mr. Jones'

'What are you doing up this early?' he said to Charlotte as his face softened.

'You only get about five hours sleep on Zopiclone' she replied.

'Are you feeling rough?'

'Yeah, very. I've done some digging around for you and the story isn't true. She didn't pay for her boob job on benefits. Actually, she works part-time. She was paid to say otherwise.'

Mr Jones, aware of Aktor's gaze promptly said 'thanks for letting me know' and ended the call.

He threw his phone onto the table and turning to Aktor said. 'I knew it. This story is made up.'

Thoughts...

Relax
If you have noticed vaginal
dryness check out water-based
lubes.
@sexwithcancer
www.lovehoney.co.uk
www.sexwithcancer.com

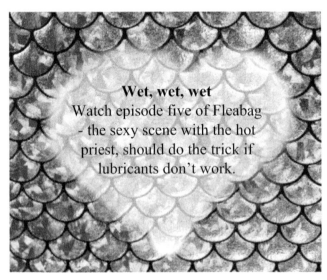

Wet, wet, wet
Watch episode five of Fleabag
- the sexy scene with the hot
priest, should do the trick if
lubricants don't work.

26: Charlotte

Early the next morning, I was lying face-down on the cold white-tiled bathroom floor. Mainlining salted crisps to stop the nausea. It was like an avalanche of chemicals had exploded in my body. Suddenly I could hear Felix getting up from his bed. Using the side of the bath, I managed to haul myself up. I didn't want him to see me, lying on the floor and become worried.

The next week passed in a chemical stupor. It was difficult to distinguish between night and day. I didn't want to eat anything. Or even drink water. I knew I had to, otherwise I would die. Some people are okay with chemo. I wasn't one of them. I was on a three-week cycle. BMW, whom I rang daily, said week one would be a week of duvet days. Week two would be feeling a bit better and week three, I'd start to pick up again ready for the next onslaught.

But week one was more like being on skid row rather than duvet days. BMW also said that I should get out in the garden and lie on a sun lounger. I could only look out the window at the sun lounger from my bed. I could eat very little, apart from crisps, but I did manage chicken soup and lime pickle straight from the jar. Apparently if you're someone who gets morning sickness when pregnant, then sickness from chemo is more likely to happen. I had severe morning sickness with both pregnancies.

A friend of a friend rang me in the middle of my chemo and said, 'How are you?' He had been a seventies rock star. I said, 'I feel terrible. I feel like I'm coming off heroin.'

'I know what that's like, coming off heroin. You're right, it's like that,' he said.

In week two I went to see a healer. He had a waiting list of a year. But I had booked him once before I left London, so he managed to squeeze me in for an appointment. Kindly, Pauline took me there. He said; 'Breast cancer is the best thing that's ever happened to you.' I started to cry because my hair was now falling out in strands, He took me aside and said, 'I'm going to give you the proverbial slap round the face.' Nice, I thought. As I clawed my hair, more and more strands were coming out.

'This isn't about what you look like,' he said. 'It's about your health. That's all that matters at the moment.'

After that, I perked up about the hair issue. I just had a little cry on the way home as the radio was playing out David Grey's *Please Forgive Me*. I felt I was a real fuck-up getting breast cancer and I'd let myself and others down. Though the hair issue certainly felt a lot better, after the healers little chat with me, I now sported a beautiful glossy wig, which I wore 24/7 to disguise my head from the children. They were too little to understand, but I really didn't want to scare them. I had enough trouble with my own fears, let alone being able to cope with them being scared. At night-time when they were in bed, I would come in and lie next to them, cuddling them individually to reassure them that Mummy was just a bit poorly. Although I was unable to reassure myself, I was so frightened. I never took my wig off. I didn't even let myself see what I looked like without hair. I thought my obsession with how ugly I looked was unhealthy.

When I experienced extreme itching under the wig, the chemo nurse reassured me it was just a reaction to the drugs and to take some antihistamine. Little did I realise, the kids had picked up nits from school and because of lying next to them at night, the headlice had crawled from their heads onto my wig and started having a blood-sucking party underneath it. The nits didn't think, oh this is a wig, we're not going to jump on this one.

It was my hairdresser, Suzy, that discovered them.

Sitting at my kitchen table I said to her, 'Look at my scalp.'

She carefully took the wig off and shrieked. 'You've got nits. You must be the first person to have no hair and have nits.'

We both laughed and she put the offending wig in a plastic bag, knotted it, and took it away to disinfect it. That night, I had the unenviable task of administering the children's nit treatment in the bath. This made me want to gag, on top of the chemo which made me want to gag anyway.

Thoughts...

Kalm your Sutra
Certain positions can be uncomfortable after breast surgery. Try lying on your side rather than your back if it helps or check out Karma Sutra books.

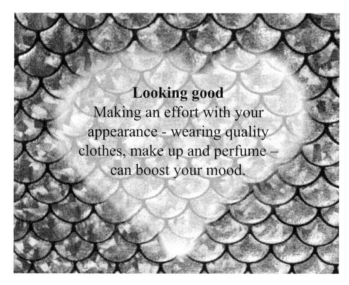

Looking good
Making an effort with your appearance - wearing quality clothes, make up and perfume – can boost your mood.

27: Charlotte

After a week of chemo, my temperature rocketed up due to an infection. You have to be really careful whilst your white blood cell count is down because you can pick up any bug which can be fatal if it's a particularly nasty one. Sam reluctantly drove me to A&E. I waited to be seen by a very harassed doctor, I was shivering as I lay in one of the trolley bays.

'Could you get me a blanket?' I asked Sam.

'No, you don't need that,' said Sam. 'The doctor will be back in a minute.'

The doctor didn't come back, and I asked again, 'Can you get me a blanket?' This time he did.

I was still feeling sick, I asked Sam to get me a packet of crisps. I was eating at least two packets a day before 8 o'clock in the morning. There was something about the salt mopping up the bleach pond in my stomach.

While Sam was gone a group of medical students appeared at my bedside, I was happy to answer their questions and show them my silicone boob which the female medical students were seriously impressed with. In the midst of this Sam reappeared clutching a bag of crisps.

'Give me five minutes,' I said to him.

He returned a quarter of an hour later. 'Could I have the crisps please?' I said,

'Oh those,' he said. 'I ate them.'

I had to be admitted because my blood cell count was dangerously low. I was now in an isolation room off the main ward being given high doses of antibiotics. I sweated all night with a fever, and dreamt that there was a Roman battle going on outside my room, due to the large amount of traffic going past. At one point I thought, a chariot missing a wheel was being dragged past my room. It was probably a bed or something being moved to another ward. After a night of very disturbed sleep, I was desperate to have a bath.

Despite my weakened state, I managed to get a towel, a bar of soap and get to the bathroom. Which was quite far down a long corridor. It was like crossing a battlefield with the all the activity going on, nurses running around and doctors' bleepers going off. I sat on the edge of the bath, reached down to put the plug in the bath and realised there wasn't a plug. I'd used up all my energy to get to the bathroom and my legs felt like jelly, carrying my own body weight seemed like such an effort. Big fat tears started dripping down my face.

Fortunately, a nurse appeared round the door a few minutes later, took pity on me and rushed off to find another bath plug. Having a bath and keeping clean was a huge challenge for me. I had to take off my wig. I was very careful not to look at my bald head, as the feeling of self-loathing was so great. But I had to wash my head at the same time. Circumnavigating the bathroom and accessing the bath was difficult too. Because taking off my clothes, and seeing myself naked was just abhorrent to me. The real challenge was not to look in the mirror on the wall next to the bath. I knew if I looked, it would all be over. That I wouldn't be able to cope. It was like looking into the witch's eye for me. If I did, I would be dead.

My courage and bravery only extended so far and the feelings would overwhelm me. I had one boob that looked like Katie Price's and the other that looked like Miss Marple's. It wasn't a good look. But worse was my extreme skinniness. The type of thinness I had wanted all my life, and now that I had it, I didn't want it. I looked like a teenager with boyish hips. I looked like a sexless android with sticking-out ribs. I didn't resemble me anymore. I finally managed to get into the bath, averting my eyes from the mirror. The hot water and soap were bliss, but I felt desperate for my mother. I felt like a child, yet I was a 40-something woman. I desperately needed my mother now and felt so alone. I started crying again. I'd have given anything to have talked to my mother. I wanted to send her a message, or I wanted her to send me a message. Then I had this feeling which was like a message, my mother saying to me, 'I'm here. I'm here for you. I've sent Pauline to look after you.' And I felt comforted when I thought of Pauline's smiling face.

As I started soaping under my arms, I felt a lump under my right armpit. It was on the left side was where I'd had the cancer; and feeling this new lump I thought it had spread to the right. Could this really be it then? Was this the end?

At that point, I heard a young nurse's voice outside the door, she asked if she could come in. I'd forgotten to lock the door, so she could. 'Are you okay?' she asked.

'No,' I wailed. 'I've got a lump under my other arm now. How has it got so much worse for me? It was bad enough anyway.'

'Sometimes, you have to go down a bit lower before you start to come back up. But I'll get a doctor to look at it for you,' she said. 'That won't be till Monday though because it's the weekend. But don't worry about it – it's probably just an ingrown hair follicle.

Don't worry about it, I thought. That's one thing I can't do.

I walked back to the ward wrapped in a towel, not knowing whether to tell Sam or not.

Twenty-four hours later, I was out of isolation and on the cancer ward. The lump had turned out to be an ingrowing hair so I didn't bother to tell Sam about it. The cancer ward was quite a grim place to be, although I had got a bed by the window, so there was some semblance of an outside world. I didn't fit in on the cancer ward. Apart from the obvious fact that I'd got cancer or had it I felt like an outsider, an intruder. I didn't even wear the uniform. I was dressed in size 10 jeans that were slipping off me and should really be a size 8, a coral hoody, a glossy wig and a modicum of make-up, mainly eyeliner and concealer. The other women eyed me from their beds as I trotted back and forth. I felt ostracised. One elderly lady said, 'You're lucky you're up and about.'

The regulation attire was an old floral night dress and a bloated face with a bald head. I sensed the other women observing suspiciously because, I didn't fit in. I felt like they hated me. But I was desperately trying to hold on to some semblance of normality, of looking normal and feeling normal. One lady Ellen, whom I got friendly with, said to me, 'When I first saw you across the ward, I thought "that poor young girl", as breast cancer can be much more progressive when you're younger.' But I was no young girl, or only at a distance. I was actually just two years younger than Ellen herself.

In the bed next to me was a mum of three who was on breathing apparatus. Her husband and children had been to see her and I had been privy to the conversation. The doctors had said that there was nothing more they could do for her and they would be moving her to the hospice. You could see the heartbreak on the children's faces, with the dad trying to be brave. Sam blundered in, in the middle of this scene and said 'What's that racket?' I pulled a face and put my finger to my lips to silence him. It was the noise of her respirator. It seems you couldn't even die in peace.

Sam sat at my bedside clutching a cream tea from the chiller in the Spar shop. 'I bought this for you,' he said looking very pleased with himself.

'I won't be able to eat that,' I said. 'I feel sick.'

'I'll have to eat it then,' he said.

'No grapes?'

That night I didn't know what to do with myself. The breathing on the respirator was getting more and more laboured. I couldn't really have a conversation with the lady because of the mask on her face. 'I hope you're okay,' was all I could say. I didn't think she could hear me, but she could read the expression on my face and she half-smiled.

I hid in the reading room with Ellen to avoid going back to the ward. Ellen had leukaemia and we bonded that night in the way that you do when you are thrown together in a difficult situation. We even broke into laughter at stories we exchanged with each other and giggled about the books in the reading room, tomes such as *Fear of Dying*, *Death and Beyond* and *Dying to Save You*. 'They've all got death in the title,' squealed Ellen.

She wore a very attractive wig and was really slim as well, so I had a buddy for that night anyway. She told me how she'd been on the beach surfing with her children. 'I was as fit as a fiddle,' she said, brown and toned, jumping in and out of the water laughing. I looked at all the pale overweight women my age sitting on the beach and I thought, you bunch of lard arses, look at me, 'I'm really fit'. That was a few days before I was diagnosed with leukaemia. Ellen died three months later, despite extensive bone marrow treatment. I attended her funeral.

****

There was an ulterior motive for me to look the best I could under the circumstances. There was always the chance that I might run into Mr. Jones, whose frank intelligence made him even more striking. And to my surprise, there was a text message from him when I got back to my bed, which read, 'Hi Charlotte. Came to see you as I was working late. Hope you're okay. Mr. Jones.'

I didn't know how he'd got my number. It was at times like those, that I really missed Natasha. I badly needed her input, and we would have dissected his text for syntax, semantics and subtext in a 'He loves me, he loves me not' fashion.

Thoughts...

I'm back bitches
I wore 'war paint' and glamourous clothes, which helped me feel better. Striding out, shoulders back, head held high, with lots of Attitude

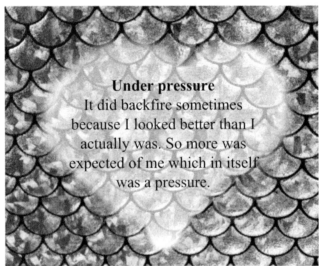

Under pressure
It did backfire sometimes because I looked better than I actually was. So more was expected of me which in itself was a pressure.

28: Damien

Damien and Jasmine were sitting side-by-side, on a fallen oak tree which was carpeted in neon green moss, in the middle of the woods that bordered the Treatment Centre. Damien had slipped a knife from the kitchen into his pocket and carved 'D for J' in a heart on the trunk. This was their spot for illicit cigarettes. They would leave group therapy separately, grab a cup of strong coffee and then head to their hideaway in the woods. The sexual tension had been building for weeks between them. Jasmine found Damien's honesty intoxicating. They would sit together on this fallen tree, thighs touching each other, sharing a cigarette, brushing their hands against each other as they did so. It was gone 6 o'clock in the evening and starting to get dark.

Nestling up to Jasmine - Damien said, 'Where do we go from here, then?'

'What do you mean?' said Jasmine.

'The thing is, I want to touch and kiss you, but you're married.'

There was a pause - and then as he leaned forward, he started kissing her on her delicate, soft neck working his way towards to her rouge-nude lips. Tantalising her with his tongue - she responded immediately - within minutes, he was tearing at her clothes and pushing her firmly up against the trunk - of a non-felled large oak - lifting her up and wrapping her legs around him he slipped his erect cock into her surprisingly tight cunt. It was frantic and all over in minutes. For Jasmine, it was the thrill of fucking a bad boy, as with her husband it was slow, considerate and meaningful. For Damien, the thrill of fucking the posh girl. They both started putting their clothes back on, realising they were going to be late for dinner and would be spotted if they didn't hurry up.

When Dick called that night, to speak to Jasmine, she sounded subdued, although in reality she couldn't sleep for excitement at the thought of meeting Jack Rashleigh and maybe going to LA.

Thoughts...

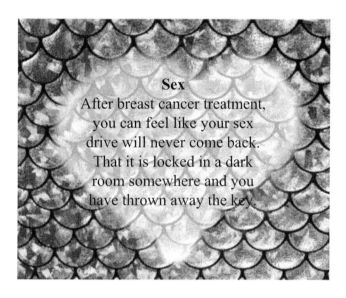

Sex
After breast cancer treatment,
you can feel like your sex
drive will never come back.
That it is locked in a dark
room somewhere and you
have thrown away the key.

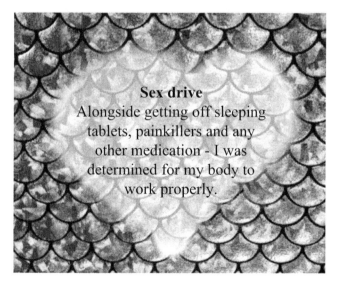

Sex drive
Alongside getting off sleeping
tablets, painkillers and any
other medication - I was
determined for my body to
work properly.

29: Charlotte

Chemo really took its toll on me but eventually it was over. My oncologist said, he would be happy for me to do four rounds but six would be preferable. There was no let-up though. Radiotherapy started the moment I finished chemo. On the first day of my radiotherapy, I was nearly in tears. I was so weak from the chemo, I felt like a rag doll. My arms and limbs flailing around as my torso took the blows.

Feeling cold was the worst part of radiotherapy – as the metal equipment pin-pointed the tattoo between my cleavage where the waves needed to hit. I was to endure this treatment every day Monday to Friday for three weeks at exactly 9.05am each day. You had to be there precisely on time or you would miss your slot as there was a queue of people behind you.

A few minutes into the treatment, I could smell burning. 'Oh my god,' I said, 'Is my flesh burning?' Although I couldn't feel any pain.

'No, my love,' said the cheery radiographer. Someone's smoking outside next to the air conditioning unit. Probably one of the surgeons.'

'I bet they don't get cancer,' I said. The radiographer laughed.

****

It was Christmas, and all the radiotherapy treatment had finished. I was now left with the decision of whether to have a second mastectomy for medical safety and aesthetics. I was chatting in the waiting room, piped music was playing Frank Sinatra's Christmas collection, and everyone was in good spirits, despite it being a breast cancer clinic. It was bit like the Germans and the English in the trenches during the First World War singing *Stille Nacht*; everyone had put aside their battle with cancer to enjoy some of the festive season. I was with my friend Nicky whom I'd met during chemo, and laughing my head off at an anecdote she was relating. I was laughing so much, I didn't notice Mr. Jones entering the waiting room and when I turned round, he was at my side clutching a package. He handed it to me. The other patients all craned their necks in amazement seeing him sit down next to me.

'Is that a Christmas present?' I said before he had a chance to answer. Then I said:

'Why have you wrapped it in gaffer tape?'

He went bright red.

'It's your notes. You'll need to take them with you when you go for your heart scan.'

I had to have a heart scan because I was being given Herceptin as well as chemo. Herceptin was the new cancer wonder drug for women with HER-2 type cancers. When Herceptin had first been launched it was a postcode lottery for the drug. People were selling their homes to buy Herceptin just to keep themselves alive.

'Only a man would wrap a present in gaffer tape.'

He took the package back and wrote 'Merry Christmas Charlotte. Love Mr Jones. Then handed it back to me, walked off with his shoulders clenched.

'You really embarrassed him,' said Nicky. 'He went sored.'

I looked at the clock and realised I had five minutes to get to my next appointment. I couldn't believe what I'd just done. I should have known it wasn't a Christmas present. The package had 'Nuclear' written on it. I went out in a hurry it was snowing and extremely windy bordering on a blizzard. In my haste I dropped the package. As I went to pick it up, all the contents fell out and started blowing around. The ink started to run on some of the letters. I started to run around like a headless chicken trying to pick up bits of paper, praying that Mr. Jones wasn't looking out of the window observing the snow globe scene. It was my god punch for embarrassing him. When I finally reached the cardiography room, I handed over the sodden notes to reception.

'Why have you brought those?' the receptionist asked. 'We don't need them.'

'Really?' I said, as my mind replayed the scene in the car park where bits of my notes were swirling around like giant snowflakes.

Two hours later I was back in the waiting room to see Mr. Jones. To my relief he didn't mention the snow scene so my pride was intact. He was hesitant. 'You've been through a rough time. How was the journey?' he asked.

'Journey?' I said, 'It was more like a ride on a bloody ghost train.'

He laughed. Then he said, 'What do you want to do about the remaining healthy breast? Have you, given it some thought?'

I'd given Mr. Jones a lot of thought but hardly given the surgery any. I felt that I was getting better though because my thoughts about death were getting less and less. When you have cancer, everyone tells you it's so important to keep positive. It's almost the unspoken rule that if you keep positive you will survive. But it's very difficult to be positive, when you're shit scared of dying. We have about 60,000 thoughts a day. I was averaging 10,000 about dying, and 50,000 about Mr. Jones I considered it an improvement, because before it had been about 50,000 about dying and 10,000 about Mr. Jones. Things were definitely improving. At least the thoughts about Mr. Jones were carnal which meant I was more alive than dead.

'The thing is,' continued Mr. Jones, 'Most women can't get their head around removing a healthy breast.'

'I can't get my head around dying,' I replied.

'Good answer,' said Mr. Jones.

Thoughts...

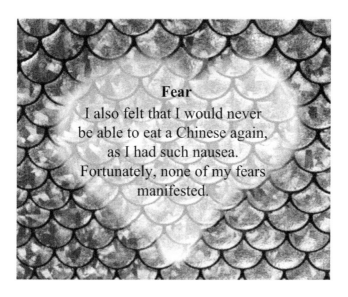

Fear

I also felt that I would never be able to eat a Chinese again, as I had such nausea. Fortunately, none of my fears manifested.

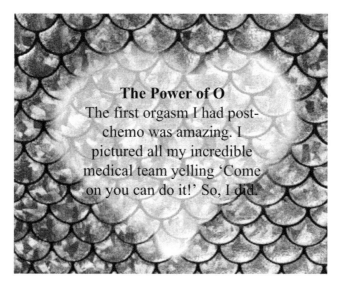

The Power of O

The first orgasm I had post-chemo was amazing. I pictured all my incredible medical team yelling 'Come on you can do it!' So, I did.

30: Damien

Damien and Jasmine were in a limo, being driven down Sunset Boulevard, courtesy of Jack's Filipino housekeeper/chauffeur, Josephine.

'I'm not going to leave here until I get an agent,' announced Damien.

'Well, I'm not going to leave here until I've done some serious shopping,' replied Jasmine.

'I should be about two hours,' said Damien. 'So, let's meet for lunch at 1pm at the Seafood bar, and hopefully I'll have something to celebrate.'

Jasmine was determined to max out all of her credit cards. By the time she got to the restaurant, her arms were being pulled out of their sockets by the designer carrier bags she hauled on either side of her petite frame. She sank into the nearest *alfresco* chair of the bistro, and ordered a glass of champagne. One wouldn't hurt after all, she'd been so good. She and Damien, apart from having a miniature vodka each, well perhaps more, on the flight from London to LA to calm their fear of flying. They hadn't drunk for twelve weeks in treatment; and were due to spend a month in a Halfway House before they could go home. But the opportunity to jet off to LA and meet The Rash presented too much of a temptation. She also lit up a cigarette. The glass of champagne felt like liquid gold as it slipped down her throat. It was the most delicious thing ever. Could things get any better? She was now able to have just one drink. The sun was shining, she was in LA and was about to meet Jack Rashleigh.

Damien appeared. 'I see you haven't wasted any time then?' he said, vying her empty glass. 'Let's get a bottle and some langoustines. I've had some good news.'

'What's that?' enquired Jasmine.

'I've just done a screen test' he said. They said I was a natural, and likely to be the next Jerry Springer. Jasmine shrieked as they clinked glasses.

****

When Damien and Jasmine got back to The Rash's mansion, there was no sign of Jack. According to Josephine, he was working late at the studios. Jasmine opened the fridge and found a bottle of Cristal champagne that had already been opened. As far as she could tell, only one glass had been drunk from it. She grabbed the bottle and a couple of flutes, jaunted off to find Damien – who was now sprawled on the bed in one of the vast monochrome suites.

'We can't waste this,' said Jasmine as she swigged from the bottle. 'It's nearly £200 a bottle, and it will go flat.'

'So much for the posh girl. Can't you use a glass?' said Damien, as he grabbed the bottle out of her hand and swigged it himself. He pulled her close and passed champagne into her mouth via his tongue, then kissed her deeply.

Jasmine climbed on top of him giggling.

They both fell asleep, naked on the bed, in the temperate Californian night.

At 2 o'clock in the morning, Jasmine woke up with a raging thirst due to the champagne she'd quaffed. She untwined her naked body from Damien's pulled on a very skimpy nightdress and padded barefoot downstairs to the kitchen where there was a dim light on.

Huge grey bifold doors extended the threshold of the kitchen into the garden, and Jack was sitting on the terrace at a table smoking a cigarette, on the phone to someone. He was even better looking in real life with his film-star looks dark brown eyes and dark floppy hair. He looked up, took her in and quickly finished his call.

'Hello, I'm Jasmine,' she said, proffering her hand.

'I'm Jack,' replied The Rash offering his.

'I need a glass of water,' said Jasmine.

Jack stubbed out his cigarette, got up from the table and went to the filter machine.

'Come and have a seat,' he said motioning to the table and chair. He could smell alcohol on her breath. 'So, tell me about you. How did you meet Damien?'

'Well, um.'

'Oh' said Jack. 'You met him in one of those funny meetings he goes to.'

'Yes, that's right.'

'Doesn't seem to be working though, does it?'

Jasmine laughed. She gradually unfolded her back story: how she'd met Mr. Jones, what a great surgeon he was, how he was at the hospital all the time and how she rarely saw her girls, as they were at boarding school. As she was telling him details of her life, he punctuated it with questions. Jasmine also asked Jack what he was like before he became The Rash.

'I was always The Rash,' replied Jack with a big grin, revealing a set of expensive veneers.

Gone 4 o'clock in the morning, they were still chatting. Jasmine was inching towards him.

'I don't understand about alcohol,' said The Rash. 'I say to Damien, "Just have one, like me".' Jack lit a cigarette and handed it to Jasmine. She put her hand on his thigh. He looked down at her erect nipples, visible through her transparent gossamer nightdress. He quickly removed her hand.

Jasmine was stunned. 'No one's ever refused me,' she said.

'Well, we've got that in common' said Jack.

'What's wrong?' she said, looking at Jack with her big doe eyes.

'What's wrong?' He said: 'You're very beautiful, and I find you very attractive but you're with Damien and you've got a wedding ring on your finger. I've got a girlfriend and you've been drinking. I think it's best you go back to bed now.'

Jasmine skulked off to bed, alongside a snoring Damien.

She'd left her mobile phone on by the side of the bed and at 6am it sprang into life. It was Dick. 'Where are you? I phoned the treatment centre and they said you'd left.'

'Oh,' said Jasmine, trying to gather her thoughts hastily. 'I'm at the Halfway House now in Kensington. I tried to call you. They're so pleased with the speed of my recovery they said I could go to Halfway. I'm supposed to spend the next month here.'

'Oh, that's great. I'm so proud of you.'

'So, how are the girls?'

'We're all missing you. Do you want a word with them?'

Jasmine had a pleasant conversation with Isobel and Mimi, asking them about school and reassuring them that she would be home soon and was feeling much better.

She put the phone down and looked at Damien, who was still fast asleep. She pulled on a fluffy white robe and went downstairs in search of some breakfast. Jack was in the kitchen, chatting to Josephine. He'd just been out for a run and smelt of clean sweat.

'Hi Jasmine,' he said, 'You're looking ravishing this morning. Would you like a smoothie?'

Josephine offered her a glass. They also had coffee, and Jasmine picked at one of the pastries which had just been delivered fresh from the bakery.

'When are you due back in London?' asked Jack.

'Well,' she said guiltily. 'We're supposed to be at a Halfway House in Kensington. The thing is, we can't go to Halfway because we've been drinking and they'll pick it up in the blood test and we'd get kicked out. But I can't go home because Dick will suss it out.'

Jack was feeling awkward about last night. 'Why don't you go and stay in my house in Chelsea? You and Damien could stay there for a week and dry out. I won't be there as I'm not due back in London till filming starts again.'

'Oh wow, that'd be great!' said Jasmine. 'I'll tell Damien.'

****

Jack's house in London was muted everything was either grey, white or black, so minimalist to the point of looking like no one lived there. There were no quirky glimpses of personal effects and each room looked like it was staged for a magazine shoot. The only signs of someone living there were fishbowls of white lilies on the extensive Italian white marble surfaces and the gargantuan fruit bowl with pineapples, watermelons, papayas and guavas. Everything had a push-button, whether it was to shut curtains or blinds, or to work the fountain in the lavish garden. Jack's Filipino maid in London, Gina, catered for Jasmine's every whim. She and Damien spent a week there fucking and shopping, fuelled by champagne.

'Have you heard back about your TV show?' asked Jasmine, one evening over dinner.

'No, no, not yet,' replied Damien.

His mobile rang and the number of the Treatment Centre flashed up. He killed the call.

'Why aren't you answering that?' asked Jasmine.

'It's the Treatment Centre.'

'What do you think they want?'

'They'll be wondering where we are.'

They would have been chasing Damien's unpaid fees too. Early on, Damien and Jasmine had been asked by the Treatment Centre if there was any way they could donate money for a new wing. All the patients had been asked if they could donate. Jasmine had asked Dick but he had said no as any money he raised had to be for the Cancer Centre. Damien had approached Jack Rashleigh, and he had offered £100k which was nothing to Jack, it was the kind of money he put in his back pocket. Damien had come up with the idea of using £50k of it to pay his treatment fees, as the Treatment Centre were really onto him now. He could tell the Treatment Centre that Jack was donating £50k and Jack would be too busy to notice. Damien gave his bank account details to Jack's accountant for the transfer. When the money hit his account, he was going to siphon off £50k for himself, and donate the remaining £50k for the new wing.

Thoughts...

Luna

I was also told after chemo that my periods wouldn't come back but they did.

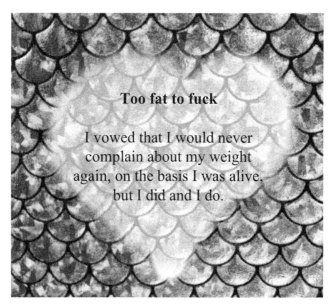

Too fat to fuck

I vowed that I would never complain about my weight again, on the basis I was alive, but I did and I do.

31: Mr. Jones

Mr. Jones picked up his razor. He was going out tonight and needed to look good. He eyed himself in the mirror. Even he realised how handsome he looked in his Jermyn Street pinstripe suit and crisp white shirt with cufflinks. But he had creases at the corners of his eyes from tiredness. He would much rather stay in tonight, spend some quality time with the girls and maybe watch a film.

Dick hated social events. He was much more a one-to-one person. Socialising was outside his comfort zone. He was comfortable in a work environment but he hated the social events connected to his work. But there were a certain number of occasions each year were he had to attend. He disliked them because he had to be Dick , rather than hiding behind Mr. Jones, the surgeon. Having Jasmine at his side always eased the way. But this time Jasmine couldn't be there. He was pleased in one way though. She had been doing so well in treatment that she had been transferred to the Halfway House in London. He was excited about her coming home soon and them being a family again.

He was more uncomfortable about this event than usual. He had been persuaded by Charlotte to get involved with a project called, *Inspirational Women.* It was a fund-raiser for the new breast cancer unit.

He'd asked Charlotte if she could write an article of her experience of breast cancer that would have highlighted the need for funding. But she'd flatly refused: 'I'm just another breast cancer story. My story's not interesting enough. You need a more interesting angle to get an editor excited. Do you remember that picture of a woman with a bald head, and a completely flat chest after a double mastectomy? That ran on the front page of the *Evening Standard?*

'Yes, I do,' Mr. Jones had replied.

'It terrified me,' Charlotte had said. 'It was such a hard image. She looked like a man. She'd lost her femininity. That image really haunted me and I was sure it would haunt other women as well. We need to have some positive images of women who've had breast cancer.'

And that was how *Inspirational Women* had come about.

Thoughts...

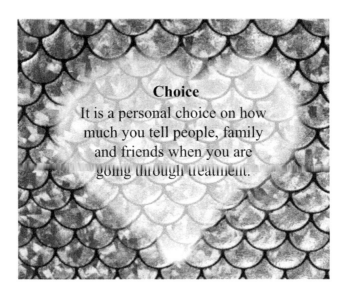

Choice
It is a personal choice on how much you tell people, family and friends when you are going through treatment.

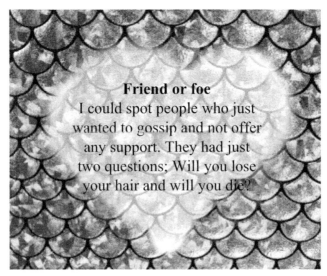

Friend or foe
I could spot people who just wanted to gossip and not offer any support. They had just two questions; Will you lose your hair and will you die?

32: Charlotte

I was nervous but excited about seeing Mr. Jones. I hadn't been out in the evening for at least a year and had spent the last twelve months in tracksuit bottoms or PJs. So, wearing a figure-hugging dress was a big deal. I hated the thought of people looking at me and feeling sorry for me. So, I needed to look good to deflect their sympathetic glances. A former female acquaintance, who had cancer 30 years prior, had told me about one female friend who, every time she saw her – which wasn't often – would cock her head to one side and say, 'Are you okay?' in a patronising tone.

I wore a bottle-green silk dress, long black boots and black tights. My hair was beginning to grow back, but I looked more lesbian than Sinead O'Connor. My gay friend, Abi, said it was different if you have the lezzer haircut by choice. I wore a glossy wig and full make-up to disguise how I actually looked and felt.

Before leaving I had a glass of wine, to settle my nerves. The gallery was teeming as we arrived and Sam immediately shot off to go and look at the view of the beach. I suddenly saw Mr. Jones approaching me, looking less than happy. He came up to me, kissed me on each cheek, and then whispered in my ear, 'I want to kill you.'

'Why? You've just saved my life!'

'The headline in your newspaper.'

Oh yeah, the article.

'Mr. Jones's Boobs,' said Mr. Jones.

'Oh god. Is that the headline they've run with? I didn't know that. What does Sir Mountford say about it?' I said, trying not to laugh.

'He's not best pleased. Would you like a drink, by the way?'

'I think I need one. The thing is,' I said backtracking like mad. 'The *Daily News*, being the biggest newspaper in the world, is going to get you the best coverage, and *Daily News* readers aren't like the Guardian lot, who know all about checking their breasts for lumps. If you could swallow your pride maybe this is a good thing?'

Mr. Jones half-smiled, his sense of humour returning as the alcohol hit his bloodstream.

The evening continued, I flitted in and out like a social butterfly. Talking to people I hadn't seen in over a year. Everyone commented on how well I looked, which boosted my confidence but thinking, they wouldn't say that if they saw me naked.

The evening culminated in the auction with pictures of each woman being projected onto the back wall. The bidding was fast and furious. Each print sold for at least £2000. By the end of the evening, £40,000 had been raised for the new cancer ward.

I was to let my hair down - even though I didn't have much. It was so exhilarating all that money being raised. I had been really worried when he had told me about the headline. I knew all those snooty medical professors wouldn't be happy about tabloid exposure. But then, you can't have it both ways. When there are lives at stake, does it matter about the coverage? I was anticipating Mr. Jones's reaction hoping he'd come and find me before Sam did. Seconds later, Mr. Jones spotted me across the crowded gallery and immediately came striding over.

'Wow,' he said. This is amazing!'

He looked so handsome, a smile so radiant. I just wanted him to take me out of sight, away from the guests, and fuck me up against the wall.

He hugged me and said, 'I can't thank you enough.' Then he said, 'There's a quiet area over there.' At that point Sam came up and Mr. Jones and I sprang apart. 'Thank you,' I said to him and shook his hand. 'It's been a great evening.'

'Yes, it has,' he said looking awkwardly at Sam.

I walked off with Sam, glancing back, wanting to mouth at Mr. Jones. 'I'm sorry', but I couldn't.

Thoughts...

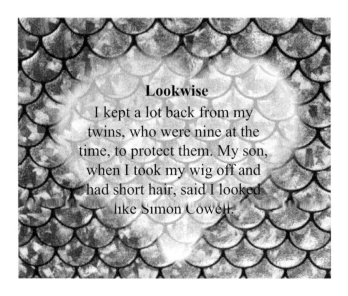

Lookwise
I kept a lot back from my twins, who were nine at the time, to protect them. My son, when I took my wig off and had short hair, said I looked like Simon Cowell.

Kids eh?
He said: 'Don't pick me up from school looking like that again.' I said 'Don't you love me unconditionally?' 'Not with that haircut' he replied.

33: Damien

Damien's hands were shaking as he lit a cigarette. He proceeded to call the Treatment Centre. The phone rang for ages until someone eventually picked it up. Damien and Jasmine had hatched a plot in the kitchen over copious cups of strong coffee from Jack's coffee machine which resembled a small steam train, it had so many attachments.

'Hi, it's Damien Rashleigh here.'

Jasmine was listening to his conversation, as she was sipping her skinny latte.

'I have some good news. I'm about to put £100,000 into the Treatment Centre's account.' Damien dragged on his cigarette, paused before his next statement. '£50,000 is to cover my outstanding fees, and £50,000 as a donation to the new wing.'

'Wow, thank you,' said Caroline, the administrator. 'I'm quite overwhelmed. I'll tell Declan.' - the main counsellor.

'If you speak to Declan,' said Damien, 'Could you explain and apologise for our absence? Myself and Jasmine were supposed to come straight to the Halfway House, but we did something very stupid. Jack invited us to LA for a short trip, and Jasmine is such a huge fan of his that I couldn't say no. I needed to see Jack in person to seal the deal. But we've both been abstaining from alcohol, going to meetings although it's been difficult at times.'

The generous donation from Jack and Damien Rashleigh covering his fees meant that Declan agreed reluctantly to them starting their Halfway House treatment, on the proviso that they both had alcohol and drugs tests before they entered. They both passed with flying colours as they had lasted two days without alcohol.

Life at The Halfway House was much less structured than the treatment centre. They were allowed a lot more freedom. It was supposed to be a bridge to normal living. After morning group therapy and one-to-ones, Jasmine would go shopping and meet Damien for lunch, coffee and cigarettes at cafés to while away the afternoon. They were sitting outside one café, three weeks into treatment at the Halfway House. Damien was in a foul mood, Stacey, when she wasn't reading Bride's magazines, had been phoning his mobile obsessively even though he had been advised at the treatment centre not to have any relationships for two years. And he hadn't heard from Charlotte.

'Would you just stop talking about my brother?' he snapped at Jasmine. 'It's like you've got Tourette's.'

'Oh, sorry,' replied Jasmine. 'But you go on about him the whole time. What about Damien the person, rather than Damien, Jack Rashleigh's brother? People only want to know you because you're a Rashleigh to get closer to your brother.'

'Do they?' said Damien. 'I never know.'

They sat in silence. Damien stubbed out and relit another cigarette without offering Jasmine one. She pulled out a copy of Hello magazine, her staple. She started thumbing through it. Her friend Topaz Delaney looked a bit *avoirdupois* in one picture. She won't be best pleased thought Jasmine.

By the time she got to the announcements page, Damien was ready to leave: 'Come on, let's go.'

'Fuck that,' said Jasmine. 'Waiter, could we have a bottle of your best Krug? We have something to celebrate.'

'Certainly, madam.'

'What? Damien's eyes played out confusion. Jasmine threw the magazine at him across the table.

'You're getting married.'

Thoughts...

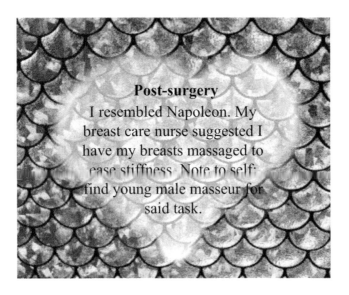

Post-surgery
I resembled Napoleon. My breast care nurse suggested I have my breasts massaged to ease stiffness. Note to self: find young male masseur for said task.

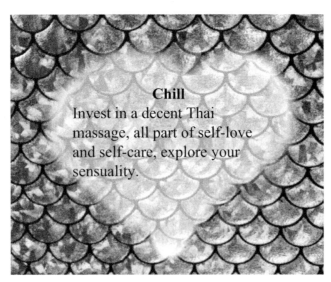

Chill
Invest in a decent Thai massage, all part of self-love and self-care, explore your sensuality.

34: Mr. Jones

It was Sunday evening, Izzy and Mimi were sprawled on the sofa, their coltish long limbs taking up most of it. Izzy was listening to her earphones, and Mimi was flicking through a gossip magazine. It was half-term they had a week off school. Dick was in the kitchen, prepping dinner. He chopped red onions and cloves of garlic, tossed them into a frying pan, opening a tin of tomatoes to fry up with diced chorizo to make a simple pasta sauce, adding fresh basil and shavings of parmigiano. He was in a good mood. Jasmine was due home from Halfway House soon, so they could be a proper family again. He was so proud of her, sticking it out in treatment and finally getting off the demon drink. Although she was allowed few visits, Dick had been able to speak to her regularly and recently she'd been in such high spirits. He could hear the excitement in her voice because she was coming home. She seemed much more like the girl he'd married. The only difficulty on the horizon was Charlotte. He had to get her off his mental to-do list…as well as his surgical list.

'Why do you read those awful magazines?' asked Dick. 'I bet you don't even know half the people who're in them. When I was your age, I was reading Shakespeare or Dickens.'

'Yeh but you were a nerd dad – oh my god,' said Mimi. 'Oh my god, I don't believe it! It just can't be, it can't be.' She started crying and screaming chucked the magazine across the room. 'It's Mum, it's Mum.'

'What do you mean, it's Mum?' said Dick. He picked up the discarded magazine and started flicking through the pages.

Mimi said, 'The picture.'

'What picture? I can't find it,' said Dick.

'Give me the magazine,' she screamed. 'There. There's the picture.'

'Oh god,' said Dick.

The headline was '*Oh Brother*', with a shot of Damien passing a cigarette to Jasmine in LA, and another picture of Jasmine kissing Jack Rashleigh goodbye on the steps of his wedding cake house in West London. The text under the photo read; 'Socialite Jasmine Jones, wife of eminent surgeon Mr Richard Jones, shares a cigarette with Damien Rashleigh.' The text under the second photograph read; 'Jasmine Jones kissing Jack Rashleigh goodbye on the steps of his home in Chelsea, Saturday morning.'

Izzy began to cry. 'Does this mean you're going to get divorced?' she said.

'No, no,' said Dick. 'Not at all. There's been some mistake here. I know the best place for that.'

With that he grabbed the magazine out of his daughter's hands, chucking it at the bin. It missed and fell on the floor. He lurched forward, grabbed it and dropped it straight into the bin, slamming the lid down.

That night after the girls had gone to bed following much reassurance, Dick crept downstairs, turned on the kitchen light and dug around in the bin to find the magazine, now spattered with tomato purée, to have another look.

'Oh fuck, fuck, fuck,' the sharp serrated edge of the discarded tin of tomatoes cut into his fleshy palm. He grabbed some kitchen roll to stop the bleeding and poured himself another glass of red wine.

He couldn't get the image of Jasmine and Jack Rashleigh fucking, her legs wrapped around The Rash, out of his mind. Jasmine wouldn't have been able to resist Jack Rashleigh. Dick went to bed exhausted every time he woke up, the images looped round his brain on a continuum. The seduction would have been slow. When Jasmine shone her light on you, you really felt the glow. Jack Rashleigh was the same, with his megawatt smile. They were in some ways the perfect match. This hurt him even more. But how did they meet? Jack Rashleigh wasn't in treatment. And how could she have been to LA? All these thoughts were whirring away in his mind, he was awake when the alarm clock went off at five-thirty.

He was due at the hospital for seven, and it was half-an-hour's drive. He couldn't face phoning Jasmine. He didn't know what to do. He didn't know what was true and what was not. He was feeling so awful, he couldn't face Charlotte either. He chastised himself for letting his guard down with her. Why does this have to happen today, of all days? he thought to himself.

He arrived at the hospital, parked in the surgeon's bay and went straight to the sluice room before anyone spotted him. He took off his glasses, splashed copious amounts of cold water onto his face. He then patted his face dry with a paper towel, blinking profusely. He cleaned his glasses and put them back on, and then strode down the corridor and met Bridget Mary Woods.

'What's wrong with you?' she asked. 'You've got a face like thunder, and what have you done to your hand?' BMW motioned him into a side room.

'Jasmine,' said Mr. Jones

BMW nodded.

'Charlotte James is first on your list.'

'Well, you can move her to the bottom of the list for starters.' He couldn't face Charlotte in the mood he was in, and wanted to clear the list of all the other patients before he got to her.

'Oh, I see,' said BMW. 'Your, not-so-favourite patient now, then,' she said, chuckling.

After putting on his theatre scrubs, he headed towards the ward. He yanked back the curtain by Charlotte's bed and with his hands on his hips said: 'You're not first on the list any more. In fact, you're last. You probably won't go down until 1 pm.'

Charlotte said nothing and Mr. Jones disappeared. Minutes later, he returned with a camera in his hand, which he placed on the cabinet next to Charlotte. Then he went into his next patient's cubicle. He started yanking Charlotte's curtain and said in front of the elderly patient in the bed 'Sorry Charlotte, I didn't mean to yank your curtain. I'm really sorry. He then looked at the lady in the bed and said, 'Charlotte knows me.'

BMW came in. Mr. Jones disappeared after seeing to his other patient, then came back with Ayaan, a trainee surgeon. Ayaan was Sri Lankan, with the biggest green eyes and the longest lashes. He resembled a deity. Mr. Jones picked up the camera and said to Charlotte, 'We need to take some shots.'

Charlotte stood there uncomfortably, whilst he was trying to take shots of her topless. She also kept looking at Ayaan.

Mr. Jones said, 'Look at me, not him.' After the photo session was finished Mr. Jones said; 'We need to get this back to a patient–doctor relationship. This is not about you looking lovely in an art gallery.' before he stalked off.

Thoughts...

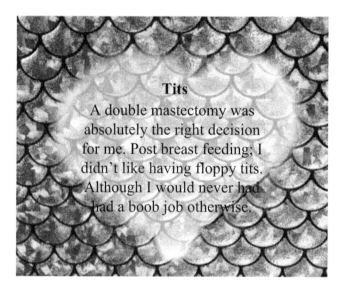

Tits
A double mastectomy was absolutely the right decision for me. Post breast feeding; I didn't like having floppy tits. Although I would never had had a boob job otherwise.

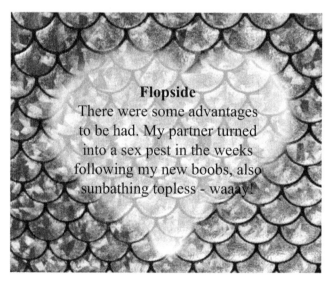

Flopside
There were some advantages to be had. My partner turned into a sex pest in the weeks following my new boobs, also sunbathing topless - waaay!

35: Charlotte

The confusing thing about breast cancer is that you have to make decisions about your treatment, at the same time as you are in a highly emotional state. All of these important decisions will affect the rest of your life or even whether you'll have a life.

Mr. Jones had said, 'The thing is, you must have an open mind about all of this. You need to make the right decision so that in ten years from now you won't have any regrets.'

Why was he saying that? I'd thought. Open mind? Does he mean I'm going to die? What does he mean I've got to make the right decision or I will die, or that I'm going to die anyway?

The wrong choice could have terrible consequences. In the end I'd realised that having a second mastectomy and reconstruction was a no-brainer. The fact that I wasn't pregnant and my lymph nodes were clear, which meant the cancer hadn't spread, lightened the load. I mean what if I'd been pregnant and the cancer had gone to my lymph nodes? Surely that would have been much harder to process.

When Mr. Jones had asked me what I wanted to do in terms of surgery, I must admit vanity had crept in. Sure, I didn't want to be told in a few months' time that the cancer had gone to the other breast, especially when staying alive for my young children was my priority. I didn't want to look in the mirror every day, and be wracked with loathing and self-obsession about odd-looking boobs. And even Sam had always said that I needed a boob job, but obviously not this way. Not that any woman was ever happy with their body, or their breasts. When I had said I didn't want one boob resembling Miss Marple and the other looking like Katie Price, Mr. Jones had laughed at me: 'Go for it, if it makes you feel better about yourself.'

In my journalist days in London, I recall interviewing a 20-year-old girl with breast cancer who was naturally quite skinny and flat-chested. At the end of the interview, she'd asked my opinion on what she should do about completing treatment for breast cancer – whether she should get her boobs reconstructed. My instant response had been, go for it, especially if it makes you feel better about yourself.

****

Very early in the morning, I was going to have the second mastectomy – or third if you count the hematoma – on health grounds; and aesthetically so that my boobs would match. Fortunately, being early summer, it was already light. I was nil by mouth, I had nothing to eat and couldn't drink any more water. Sam had to take the children to school, so at 6am I faced the lonely drive. But what was really bothering me, was not the mastectomy, although really it should have been, but Mr. Jones seeing me without a wig. By then I had short hair and felt hideous. A real contrast to the last time I'd seen him at the art gallery. I didn't think I could wear a wig in the operating theatre, and anyhow it would have been so much worse to have come round and find my wig had come off. So, I was going wigless.

Driving to the hospital, I got stuck behind a tractor - which seemed to be going at a snail's pace and started panicking about the time. This would never have happened in London I would be stuck on the Tube instead I mused.

There was nothing on the road ahead for miles, and eventually I decided to overtake. For some reason the tractor driver decided to move out at the same time, and I smacked my car into the moving parts of the tractor. There was a cracking noise, but fortunately the windscreen remained intact, all but a little chip. I hoped it wasn't going to shatter the whole windscreen, because then I'd be really done for. But I thought I was done for anyway. I couldn't cope with what I'd got to face. My heart was shattering into a million pieces. I wished someone else was doing the operation, not Mr. Jones.

The tractor driver moved off and I pulled in at the next available point. I burst into tears and slumped over the steering wheel. I stayed there motionless for about five minutes. I rubbed the tears which with the lack of sleep - made my skin feel parched. I glanced at my watch. I really was going to be late now. Miraculously, I made up speed and got to the hospital for exactly seven. BMW greeted me on arrival.

'I warn you now,' she said. 'He's in a foul mood.'

I was sitting up in the hospital bed feeling self-conscious with my lack of hair. My head was pounding from lack of food and fluids. Mr. Jones came striding over. Our eyes met and I smiled at him, but he just looked at me with disdain with his hands on his hips.

'Don't think you're going first.' he said.

'You probably won't go down until one.' I pulled my hoody over my head, and curled up into the foetal position in the bed. Meanwhile Mr. Jones started yanking the curtain that adjoined the lady in the bed next to me.

'Sorry Charlotte,' he kept repeating as he yanked the curtain even more. 'Charlotte knows me,' he said to the other patient.'

I put in my earphones and shut my eyes, hoping this horrible scene would go away. A few minutes later Mr. Jones came back and crashed the camera down onto my bedside cabinet, I jolted. Then he said, 'This is Ayaan, my trainee surgeon.'

'I was thinking about you whilst having my breakfast this morning,' said Mr. Jones.

'Lucky you,' I replied.

I thought to myself, I would give anything to eat a bowl of muesli, the blood sugar level in my body was spiraling downwards. My head was screaming.

'We need to get this back to a patient–doctor relationship,' said Mr. Jones.

I knew his subtext. He just wanted to get rid of me. I'd looked okay in the art gallery but now I looked hideous. He just confirmed it. I wished I was wearing my wig. Worse, whilst feeling so uncomfortable, I now had to have pictures taken of me topless. I pulled down my gown. I couldn't even stand upright, I was so busy clutching my gown, so it wouldn't fall to the floor. I didn't want the two men to see my knickers as well.

'Oh, you've gone all timid,' snapped Mr. Jones.

I said 'you bastard' silently to myself. Mr. Jones started taking the pictures and I gazed at Ayaan, who was beautiful.

'Look at me, not him,' said Mr. Jones. I started giggling.

Thoughts...

I will survive
Breast Cancer survival is
improving and has doubled in
the last 40 years in the UK.

www.cancerresearchuk.org

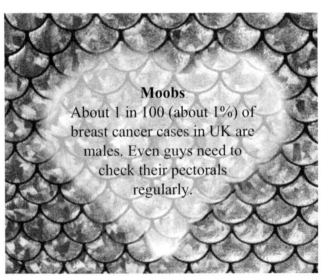

Moobs
About 1 in 100 (about 1%) of
breast cancer cases in UK are
males. Even guys need to
check their pectorals
regularly.

36: Charlotte

What had I done…What had I done? The pain in my right side was excruciating. It was as if I'd had the surgery without anaesthetic. And all for the sake of how I'd look in the mirror. I temporarily forgot the medical advantage. Sam was sitting at my bedside; I thrashed about in pain. He just looked on anxiously, rooted to the spot.

'Get the nurse,' I hissed. He wandered off in the wrong direction. It seemed like an eternity until he came back with her.

'I need pain relief.' The nurse quickly administered this.

Sam handed me a packet of biscuits: 'I thought you might like these.' he said.

The morphine kicked in and within a few minutes I was smiling at Sam I no longer wanted to kill him.

****

It was Saturday morning and the ward was empty. I managed to shuffle to the bathroom and have a bath, helped by the nurse. As I was walking back, Mr. Jones came into the ward. At first, I didn't recognise him. He was looking boyish in jeans and a T-shirt. His mood was light with no trace of yesterday's foul humour.

'You should be wearing a bra,' he said. 'You've just had breast surgery.'

'Give her a break,' said the nurse. 'She's just had a bath.'

'Oh, okay,' said Mr. Jones, sounding a bit sheepish.

We chatted for what seemed forever.

Mr. Jones was perched on the window sill by my bed until he said, 'I must go. I shouldn't really be here.'

'No, you shouldn't,' I smiled.

As Mr. Jones turned to go, Jackson Browne's *Stay* started playing in my head, and as he walked past the nurses' station, they started singing the chorus. The anaesthetic was still very much in my system.

Thoughts...

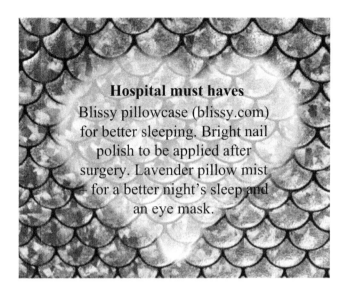

Hospital must haves
Blissy pillowcase (blissy.com)
for better sleeping. Bright nail
polish to be applied after
surgery. Lavender pillow mist
for a better night's sleep and
an eye mask.

Distraction
Audio books (Audible.co.uk)
escapist novels, memoirs and
sleep meditations.
Comedy French and Saunders
Titting About.

37: Mr. Jones

It was Saturday morning Mr. Jones was striding down the colourless hospital corridor in casual clothes, his trainers squeaking at every step. The corridor, which normally smelt of disinfectant, was unusually sweet and fragrant. He felt a stab in his chest, as it reminded him of Elizabeth Arden, the scent of his mother combined with the scent of his wife. The combination he found intoxicating. He turned left into the ward spotting Charlotte's vacated bed, surrounded by vases of lilies everywhere he looked. The aroma overpowered him and he felt tears pricking his eyes. Charlotte was nowhere to be seen and there was a card on her bedside cabinet. He went out into the corridor and checked there was no one coming. Then went back into the ward and picked up the card. His hands were shaking as he began to read it: *To Charlotte. Get well soon. The Rash x.*

He put it down immediately. Charlotte walked into the ward gingerly with the nurse by her side. Dick felt irritated as she wasn't wearing a bra. But he smiled at her.

'I thought I'd walked into a florist,' he said. 'Who are all these lilies from? Your husband?'

'No,' said Charlotte. 'Jack Rashleigh.'

'Oh, really?' said Mr. Jones his eyebrows raised and shoulders stiffening.

'Oh, it's not like that,' she said, 'I know his brother. Jack's devoted to his girlfriend. He's really loyal.'

'Is he? When he's surrounded by all those beautiful women?'

'Yes.'

****

Mr. Jones knew that he needed to confront Jasmine about those photographs. He was satisfied that Charlotte was okay, if he was honest to himself, she had been a distraction from Jasmine. When he had first laid eyes on Charlotte, he had wanted her to be okay. For her to have just a lumpectomy and nothing more than that. But when things had developed and she needed more invasive surgery and adjuvant treatment, whilst he wouldn't admit to himself that he was anything but concerned, there were certain advantages. It meant he could get to know her better which with Jasmine out of the fray seemed very appealing.

Pulling up outside his house, he noticed Jasmine had left a message on his mobile whilst he was in the hospital.

'Hi Dick,' she said. 'I'm missing you so much, but it's not long now. Only a couple of weeks. I can't wait to be back home with you and the girls. By the way, there's some stupid picture of me circulating in the gossip magazines, saying I'm in LA. I wish I was. It's a really basic existence here in Halfway. I also want to tell you, that we have a buddy system here and I've buddied up with, of all people, Damien, who's Jack Rashleigh's brother. He's promised me tickets for the girls, front row at the JR Show. I've just spoken to them and they're so excited. I've also met Jack Rashleigh. He's very charming. One thing I feel really bad about, which I know I should tell you, especially in your line of work – I've been smoking. I know you hate smoking, and will think I'm a complete idiot for doing it, but my excuse is that practically everyone smokes here. It's instead of drinking. Anyway, speak to you soon. Love you.' She ended the call. Dick listened to the message again, he felt a huge sense of relief and also sudden guilt for his preoccupation with Charlotte.

****

Dick hated the idea of couples counselling, and couldn't fit it in with his busy workload. The treatment centre had suggested it; Dick knew there would be temptation for Jasmine when she returned home. Whatever had gone on with Jasmine, Damien and Jack Rashleigh, he really didn't want to know. She was sober, and that was all that mattered.

Thoughts...

Have a laugh

Watch back-to-back episodes
of Friday Night Dinners
Netflix or whatever makes you
giggle.

Do the Tao

Every night listen to Wayne
Dyer's
5 minute meditation on
YouTube.

38: Damien

Damien and Stacey were making plans for their wedding in two months' time.

'Stacey, it's Damien. Call me back.'

The second he put down his phone, it lit up with Stacey's name: 'Hello, Mr. Rashleigh, how's it going? I tried on my dress today.'

'Excellent Darling, I've got some good news too. Jack's going to be guest of honour, and doing pictures.'

'How much for the pictures? We can go on honeymoon! Have a honeymoon, baby?'

'Jack insists that if he's to be guest of honour, the money must be given to a pet charity.'

Silence.

'Hi, are you still there?'

'Yes.'

'I've even got a date out of them.'

'Really?' shrieked Stacey.

'Four weeks tomorrow at Chelsea Registry Office. They had a cancellation and I mentioned Jack would be there.'

'But I thought we were getting married in Cornwall?'

'You can either have… Cornwall and no Jack, or London and Jack.'

Stacey went quiet again.

'Tell me about this wedding dress, because I've got to go in a minute.'

'I'm not allowed to.'

'Oh yes.'

'It's too tight. I'd better go and buy some *Slim – Fast* if I've only got four weeks.'

'Love you.' 'Love you too.'

Thoughts...

Stress factor

Big changes in life can be harsh on your health; take a step back, breathe and take one step at a time.

Breakthrough
Forget about PTSD, think post- traumatic breakthrough, when you can turn your challenging life event into something positive.

39: Damien

Things between Damien and Jasmine had cooled somewhat since the wedding announcement in *Hello*. Certainly, no more semi-naked sex sessions in the woods. Although there were no woods in SW7, there were hotels in abundance but Damien had no money. Since the announcement, Jasmine was no longer happy, despite her perceived wealth, to pay for everything.

'Why are you marrying her, and why didn't you tell me?' Jasmine asked him over coffee in South Ken, the day before they were due to leave Halfway House.

'I didn't think it would come up so soon.'

'I thought you two were just drinking buddies?'

'We are. I can't talk to her like I can with Charlotte.'

'Then you're marrying the wrong person.'

'You think I don't know that.'

'Why then are you doing it? She's not pregnant?'

'No, I've had the snip.'

'Oh yes. She doesn't know that.'

'It's to do with business.'

'Business?'

'I've had a couple of lean years, some investments that didn't pay off.'

'Well, you can't be marrying for money. Stacey's hardly an heiress.'

'Takes one to know one.'

40: Charlotte

The trouble with a cancer diagnosis and the role of 'holy cow' is that lay people become all weird around you: falsely jolly or morbidly fascinated with gory details of hair loss or boob loss. Doctors, on the other hand, post diagnosis, find a tenuous link to cancer from even the most innocent of symptoms such as a scratch or a spot. And an aching big toe requires a top-to-toe - quite literally - MRI scan.

This was how I ended up, following a brief call to my GP, watching my derriere many times magnified – so the nurse reassured me – on a large screen, surrounded by a gaggle of 12-year-old-looking boy medical students. Yes, my bum really does look big in this. But there was worse to come.

Medics call it a colonoscopy. I call it a camera up your bum. I had taken the painkiller codeine post-surgery, which was renowned for causing an internal go-slow, resulting in the passing of shards of glass and subsequent, er hem, rectal bleeding. Oh, joy of joys, a visit to the bum doctor.

What I didn't know until I saw the names on the whiteboard, was that Mr. Jones's clinic was also on a Tuesday, and that he and the bum doctor shared the same waiting room. Two strips of green plastic chairs. I sat away from the designated chairs on a strip of blue ones to ponder my predicament.

'Don't sit there, young lady – you won't be seen,' said the larger-than-life nurse.

'I don't want to be seen,' I wanted to shout back.

There's only one thing worse than being spotted in a waiting room going to see the bum doctor. I concluded, and that's being spotted stalking your surgeon. At that moment I heard Mr. Jones voice in the corridor, I darted into the Ladies. In the mirror, I looked like a startled rabbit with minimalist make-up due to this morning's small-boy-shoe-disappearing episode which had eaten up any window of opportunity for me to apply anything more than eyeliner.

Mr. Jones was nowhere to be seen I finally plucked up courage to exit the Ladies when the nurse in the waiting room called my name. I shot into a side room as she held the door.

'You're in a rush to see the bum doctor?'

'Yes, I've been really waiting for this appointment,' I winced.

When it was finally over, I nearly ran out of the hospital. I'd got away with it.

Thoughts...

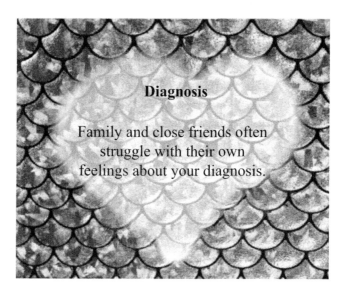

Diagnosis

Family and close friends often
struggle with their own
feelings about your diagnosis.

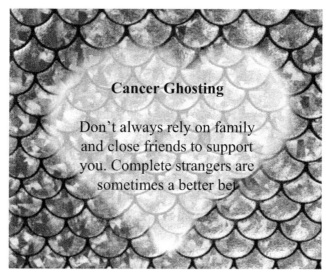

Cancer Ghosting

Don't always rely on family
and close friends to support
you. Complete strangers are
sometimes a better bet

41: Damien

It was a glorious Cornish summer's day outside, pushing 20 degrees, with a cloudless blue sky. The streets were empty, the local beaches undoubtedly packed. Damien was sat hunched up in the corner of the pub, nursing his second Jack Daniels. The pub was dimly lit to disguise the peeling paint on the walls and the ground-in stains on the swirly-patterned carpet. There was still a faint smell of cigarettes despite the smoking ban implemented a lifetime ago.

Damien liked this pub, even though it was the other side of town and he had to drive to it. There were plenty of other pubs in town; he could go to on foot. But he got left alone here, plus it was situated a couple of roads from Charlotte's house so he could keep an eye on her. He was always careful to park out of sight down a back street.

A week out of treatment, he had every reason to drink, he thought. He had a call from Jack. Everything had been going well. *Hello* magazine was paying upwards of £60k for unlimited coverage of the wedding which would be paid directly to him. But Jack wanted the money to go to a pet charity. Damien could square this somehow and then the £60k would go towards his IVA. It was the second IVA he'd reneged on; and he was being threatened with bankruptcy.

He didn't want to upset his mother, or embarrass Jack. The press would have a field day: 'No bail out for Rash's brother' with a picture of Jack on his yacht, next to a picture of Damien carrying a Poundland bag or eating out of a bin before it was fashionable - which he had done when he was homeless. Damien listened to Jack's message again:

'Sorry to leave a message: filming's behind schedule for my new show. I won't be able to make it to you and Charlotte … I mean Stacey's wedding. I thought I'd better give you the heads up now. Speak to my PA, and she'll send you two return tickets to LA for your honeymoon unless you've organised something else.'

Damien deleted it and called Stacey.

She picked up immediately, 'Hello, husband-to-be,' almost purring.

'We need to talk.'

'What's wrong? You sound awful!'

'I'm fed up with the lying.'

'What do you mean?'

'I can't go through with this wedding. I'm in love with Charlotte.'

'You bastard!' Unbeknown to Stacey, *Hello* magazine would only be interested if Jack Rashleigh was present at wedding. No Jack, no deal.

Thoughts...

Let the dust settle
Before you make any big changes, like getting married, divorced, quitting your job, do a geographical. Let life calm down a bit. Give yourself two years.

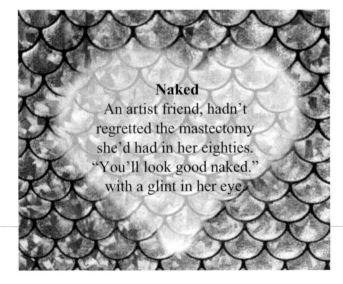

Naked
An artist friend, hadn't regretted the mastectomy she'd had in her eighties. "You'll look good naked." with a glint in her eye.

42: Charlotte

Morocco had always been my favourite place. We had honeymooned in the over-powering heat of Essaouira, one of the best anchorages off the Moroccan coast in North Africa. We had a two-storey riad, with a rooftop pool to ourselves which boasted colourful mosaic fountains, tall green exotic palms and discrete maids bringing spicy tagines and overly sweet mint tea. Wall-to-wall sex and a lot of rubbing cream into sunburnt bodies helped pass the time.

When Sam's parents offered to look after the children so we could have a long weekend in Marrakesh, I was happy. But Sam pulled a face when I told him when he came home from work.

'We can't leave the kids,'

'Why not? It's only for a weekend.'

'A long weekend. It's too much to ask of my parents.'

'Your mum wouldn't have offered if it was too much.'

'What about my dad his back is not too good?'

'*But it is only for a long……………,*' I chucked the tea towel into the Butler sink and ran upstairs.

****

We touched down in Casablanca before landing at Marrakesh. Despite the 1942 movie, Casablanca was not the most salubrious place in Morocco.

Sam had been quiet for most of the flight but then he wasn't the most relaxed flyer. As soon as we got airside, he kept checking his phone.

'They'll be fine,' I whispered in his ear before planting a kiss on his cheek. He brushed me away. He never did like PDAs, I thought.

This pretty much set the tone for what turned out to be a sex-less holiday. But I was determined to have a good time.

'It's been a tough year,' he said.

'I need time to adjust.'

One extremely arid afternoon I left Sam on the sun lounger talking to his work colleague, Will. Why did he want to take work calls when we're in Morocco? and got a decrepit taxi up a long dusty incline to the hammam.

The scent of rose oil and orange blossom was intoxicating as I entered the inconspicuous crumbling hammam. I was shown to a candlelit oasis of calm where I was laid out on a marble slab covered in soft white towels, scattered in rose petals by two women wearing hijabs.

The two women started the gomage, then they massaged my tired aching body which began to give up control. Who needs sex? I thought.

I was just about to drift off when one of the women started making circular movements round my breasts. I almost had to stop myself from jumping up and explaining why I had a boob job:

'Je suis pas putain a l'ouest, c'etait un cancer de sein.'

As Mr. Jones had done such a good job you could barely tell it was reconstructive surgery.

Thoughts...

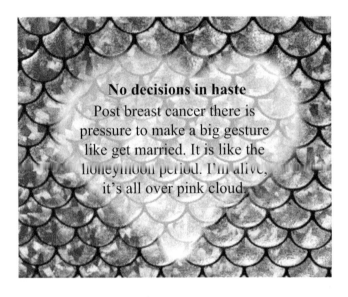

No decisions in haste
Post breast cancer there is
pressure to make a big gesture
like get married. It is like the
honeymoon period. I'm alive,
it's all over pink cloud.

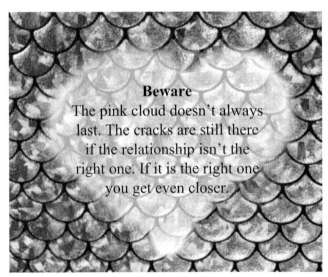

Beware
The pink cloud doesn't always
last. The cracks are still there
if the relationship isn't the
right one. If it is the right one
you get even closer.

43: Charlotte

A month had passed, and I was back at the hospital waiting for a follow-up appointment with Mr. Jones to make sure everything had healed properly. All thoughts of bum doctors had been banished from my mind as I'd been given the all clear on that front.

I dutifully changed into the neatly-folded gown BMW had given me, hugging my arms across my body for warmth. I perched on the couch in anticipation. Moments later Mr. Jones strolled in, looking taller and fitter than ever, with no hint of middle age on his neat torso. He took one look at me and said: 'So you've seen the bum doctor?'

I looked at BMW and she started laughing. Mr. Jones did too.

'Anyway, moving on,' he said as he opened my file. 'Oh, I didn't know that was in there.' He pulled a face and turned the file round so I could see. Blown up in full colour was a part of my anatomy I'd never been acquainted with before.

As I leant forward to get a closer look, I lost my balance and fell off the couch and face-planted into Mr. Jones's lap. He pulled me up and for a nanosecond we struggled to get upright and looked like we were locked in an embrace.

'What are you two like?' chuckled BMW.

Embarrassment and deep shame swept over me, like a circuit board, lighting up every visceral experience I had ever had. My body sweated with heat and shivered with cold alternately. I steadied myself, gripping the edge of the couch before propelling myself onto it to stop falling again.

There was one experience that kept flashbacking into my consciousness. An experience I'd never told anyone. Even a thousand Hail Marys (I was raised Catholic) in recompense wouldn't have cut it.

It was Sunday morning I must have been about 10. I was sitting on a hard wooden pew, feeling tired (at being dragged out of bed some ungodly hour to attend Mass) I was hungry and cold. I was in such a rush my Dad was hollering at me to get in the car. I didn't have time for breakfast and always forgot how chilly the church was even in Summer.

I was still sucking my thumb at that age, much to my parents' disgust but I would do it out of their view. They would routinely lag my thumb with *Stop & Grow* which was for nail biting and tasted disgustingly bitter. But recently I'd found something much more enjoyable than thumb sucking.

I put my hand between my thighs, and rhythmically started moving my finger under my skirt experiencing what began as small bubbles of pleasure.

I stopped immediately, when my father started coughing so badly that we were forced to leave abruptly; my father yanking me down the steps of the church so hard I thought my arm would come out of its socket.

When we arrived home, I was made to stay in my room for the rest of the day.

I felt angry and humiliated I knew I'd done something really terrible, just by the look of disgust on my father's face - which would be etched in my mind forever. But why hadn't my mother told me? This is how the conversation went a previous day in the kitchen when my dad wasn't around.

'Mum, when I touch myself should it feel fizzy and nice?'

My mother just stared out the window into the garden, she carried on washing up, clattering pots and pans. It was never spoken about again.

****

Mr. Jones, regaining his composure said: 'That's a perfectly healthy …'

'Good, good,' I replied. Then I added: 'It's okay for you medics, you're used to this sort of thing. By the way, how does it work? Isn't every junior doctor queuing up to be the boob doctor and the list for the bum doctor is hard to fill?'

'I've done boobs and bums.'

'Yes,' I replied, 'and I know which you prefer.'

'That photograph really shouldn't have been in there,' Mr. Jones reiterated, ignoring my comment.

'So, you said. Well, when I become the next JK Rowling please don't sell my picture. As they'll run with the headline: *She's an arsehole!*

After we had all stopped laughing. Mr. Jones said, 'Your picture's safe with me.' He kissed me lightly on the cheek and left the room.

Thoughts...

Have some 'Me' time

If your relationship does break up, try and have some time on your own. Rather than operate a revolving door policy.

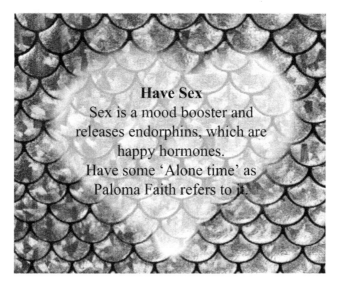

Have Sex
Sex is a mood booster and releases endorphins, which are happy hormones.
Have some 'Alone time' as Paloma Faith refers to it.

44: Charlotte

'I'll see you in six months,' Mr. Jones had said. How would I get through six months without seeing him? I thought about him night and day. I didn't really know if he liked me, apart from the fact he found me amusing, especially my visit to the bum doctor and that could be all. And now, he'd just got that awful memory of the picture to remind him of me. I wish Natasha had been here; although she'd had a crush on him as well as my husband, she would just encourage me to chase after him, I thought, knowing her.

I decided I'd just got to throw myself into family life, be a good mum and wife. Sam and I had been under a lot of pressure; I'd done things out of character. I would forget about Mr. Jones and in six months' time ask to see another consultant, Mr. Khan preferably.

I was going to have to face the playground again. Lizzie, my neighbour, had kindly been doing the school run for me alongside her two girls until I was up to it. But I felt I'd never be up to it. It sounds so silly to be scared of something so mundane as going into a playground. 'You're going to have to talk me down, to get me in the playground,' I'd said on the phone to Lizzie.

She just laughed.

'Keep your mobile at the ready,' I said.

'You're not alone, just think of all those vodka mums on the school run and how awful they must feel.'

'Yes, I've interviewed them. It wouldn't work for me. I've only drunk vodka once, on an empty stomach in Paris. Aged 16, I threw up in my French exchange girl's bed. I feel sick just thinking about it.'

The day finally came when I could put it off no longer. I had slapped on the cake-up – make-up - so much so that Lizzie, when she saw me, asked if I'd been to the Caribbean. I also sported a freshly-shampooed and styled wig.

Approaching the school gates, I had jelly legs, which morphed into the ministry of silly walks. I fell at the first hurdle, metaphorically speaking. When Sophie's TA, Angela, a woman in her sixties, spotted me, I tried to thank her as she'd really helped Sophie with her reading, but she looked at me in horror and scuttled off.

The children were spilling out into the playground. I spotted Felix first, in his black waterproof coat and waved. In keeping with school safeguarding rules, I had to wait until Felix was dismissed by the handsome Mr. Seward, the English teacher, who was on playground duty. All the school mummies adored Mr. Seward, but he was best remembered for his wife turning up at school and throwing all his clothes into the playground. He was cheating on her with a particularly attractive supply teacher. Nevertheless, he could still fill his list of mummy helpers on a school trip in a nanosecond.

As Felix was let go and crossed the playground towards me, I noticed something black stuck to the Velcro of his coat as he got nearer - smiling obliviously. He passed Mr. Seward, who said 'Bye Felix,' then looked at me and clocked my pained expression. Without Felix seeing, he swooped in, grabbed the black item and stuffed it into his pocket. He came towards me sporting a grin and said: 'I believe these are yours,' handing me my laundered black lacy knickers.

Oh, Tasha why did you have to die? How I longed for a tea and cake session with her, just to dissect the playground humiliation with Mr. Seward. Even her taking 20 wafer-thin slices of cake, instead of one whole piece, would be endearing rather than annoying. She would have laughed big belly laughs, accusing me of planting my knickers, knowing he was on playground duty. That was the sort of thing she would do.

I remembered the last Christmas BC (Before Cancer) and sadly Tasha's last Christmas. When she'd dragged me to see the gypsy, who was pure Romany and had set up shop on the piazza for the whole month of December. Tasha was obsessed with horoscopes, psychics and all manner of fortune tellers. It wasn't really my thing, but with two glasses of festive champagne sloshing round my stomach, I was game for anything.

The gypsy's caravan was warm and cosy, it had smelt vaguely of tobacco. All the soft furnishings were 1970s, a mixture of brown and beige florals. 'Sit down,' he said, pointing to a cushioned area with a static Formica table. As I handed over £20, he took the palm of my hand: 'You'll live to a ripe old age. You won't die of cancer or anything like that.'

'Great – I don't want to get cancer.'

He looked away, then back to me: 'You're not with your soulmate.'

'No, he just hurt me. But I'm happily married now.'

'No, you're not.'

'Really?'

'You haven't met your soulmate yet.'

'Really? What's he like?'

1. He's not from down here (I could hear Natasha's imaginary voice: what's the bad news?)
2. He's younger than you (Natasha: yippee!).
3. I can see him in a suit (Natasha: great!).
4. He likes to be in charge (Natasha: yes please!).
5. He's a ladies' man but doesn't act on it. (Natasha: mmm, flirty).
6. He needs to sort himself out (Natasha: a challenge).
7. He's your soulmate (Natasha: yeah).
8. He'll be totally there for you (Natasha: a *man*?)
9. He knows you're with someone (Natasha: jealous?)
10. Don't run after him (Natasha: difficult not to).

Tasha, who'd gone in after me, had been furious when I told her what the gypsy had said about my so-called soulmate: 'Your soulmate sounds like Luke.'

'But Luke's from down here.'

'Are you sure he hasn't mixed us up, crossed channels etc? He said I'd stay married and living with Mike till death us do part. That feels like a life sentence.'

'Oh Tasha,' I'd said, giving her a big hug, 'It's just a bit of fun. Don't take it as Gospel.'

Thoughts...

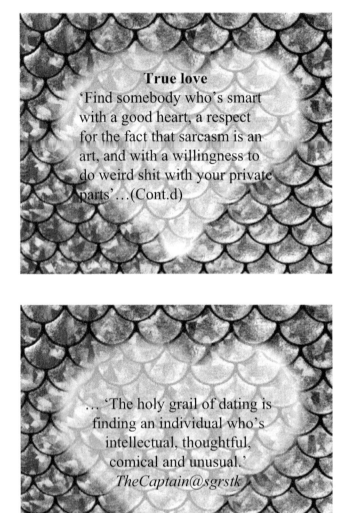

True love
'Find somebody who's smart
with a good heart, a respect
for the fact that sarcasm is an
art, and with a willingness to
do weird shit with your private
parts'...(Cont.d)

... 'The holy grail of dating is
finding an individual who's
intellectual, thoughtful,
comical and unusual.'
TheCaptain@sgrstk

45: Charlotte

The last day of autumn plus three weeks of back-to-back radiotherapy came and went. I felt shivery and my joints ached. Although radiotherapy was a walk in the park compared to chemo, it still leaves you battle fatigued and feeling vulnerable.

I just wanted to get home, light the wood burner and curl up on the sofa with a blanket and a cup of cinnamon tea. I had this tendency to over schedule myself pre-cancer, never having any breathing space, this character trait wasn't going to disappear overnight.

I had agreed to meet my cancer buddy - Nicky, at *Look Good Bald* (as I referred to it) where donations of products and make-up from the cosmetics industry were given out to cancer patients along with a make-up tutorial.

I had very little interest in make-up before cancer; I would have balked at going to something like that. But I couldn't bunk off because I had promised Nicky I would come. There was also the realization that, the more make-up you wore, the less people felt sorry for you. Especially when you looked like someone out of Belsen or the Teletubbies – it could go either way.

I was the last to arrive; everyone was already seated. Nicky squealed with delight when she saw me coming. We did pre-Covid air kissing.

"Sit down, we're about to start," said Marjorie - the larger than life, heavily made-up with what only could be described as clown-makeup group leader.

"Let's go round the room and introduce ourselves. Let's have a discussion about what we want to get out of this session or anything to do with make-up really."

Looking straight at me, she said: "Do you want to start?"

"No, but I will. My name's Charlotte. I know very little about make-up apart from the fact that I need some. I used to marvel at girls at school who caked on foundation. Wondering who they were under all that orange layering, I thought, I will wait till I'm older to wear foundation when I shall need it. Like now only now I'm too busy. I did have a makeover at Harvey Nichols once, but ended up looking like an ageing prostitute-cum-clown."

Everyone laughed, except Marjorie.

I needed the ladies, so I made my excuses and headed out the door followed by Marjorie's assistant.

"I'll show you the way, you have to go to the mezzanine level."

"Thanks," I replied.

"How long have you been doing this?" I asked.

"This is my first time. My husband had cancer."

"Is he OK now?"

"No, he's dead."

Thoughts...

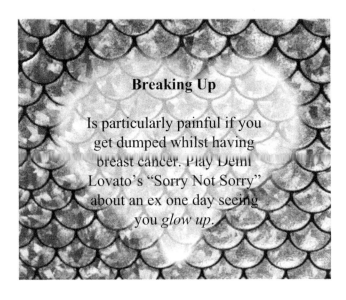

Breaking Up

Is particularly painful if you get dumped whilst having breast cancer. Play Demi Lovato's "Sorry Not Sorry" about an ex one day seeing you *glow up*.

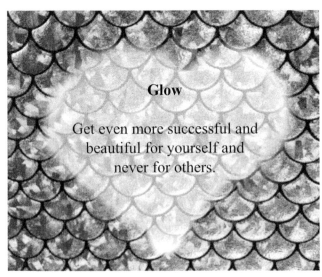

Glow

Get even more successful and beautiful for yourself and never for others.

46: Charlotte

Six months later

'I'm going to refer you for an MRI scan,' said Mr. Jones

'Really?' As a claustrophobic-hypochondriac, this was the last thing I wanted to hear.

'Just to be on the safe side and to make sure we haven't missed anything.'

The morning of the MRI scan rolled around way too soon. Sam agreed to drive me there. We sat in silence interspersed with Sam swearing at holidaymakers in the wrong lane. As we pulled up outside the clinic, Sam leant across, kissed me and said:

'Good luck, call me when you're finished.'

'You're not coming in with me?'

'You never said you wanted me to come in with you.'

'I do want you to come in with me.'

'But I'm not in the right clothes.'

'The right clothes?'

'Well, I don't feel comfortable wearing shorts in there.'

'I expect if you asked the women waiting for a scan, whether they felt comfortable in their head scarfs? They would say no.'

'I'm also meeting Will.'

'What's this obsession with Will?' I thought to myself.

My teeth were chattering, my hands were trembling as I eased myself into position; lining my body up with the giant scanner and head rest.

As soon as the whirring and clanging started, the space age capsule enveloped me, I shut my eyes and started meditating. I had headphones in, so I couldn't hear anything. I felt peaceful as the repetitive but familiar sound of my mantra soothed me.

I was just on the cusp of dropping off when a cacophony of local radio jingles blasted into my ears.

The news that day was the surprise split between singer/songwriter Edison and his model wife, Summer. Another celebrity couple bites the dust. The story transported me back to newspaper land and a story about cancer when I was working for *The Daily News*. Every year prestigious teenage bands got together to perform at London's Albert Hall to raise money for a teenage cancer charity aiming to fund the cost of teenagers having their own ward, rather than be stuck on an adult or children's ward.

I had just filed my copy which comprised of awe-inspiring interviews from three teenagers and photographs of their bald, post-chemo heads. When I had gone back to interview them face-to-face, at the Houses of Parliament, they were not recognisable from those stark pictures of when they were ill. It was a joy to see them now so healthy and vibrant.

I had pulled a quote from band front man, Edison, from the press release which ran something like this:

'We, as a band, are fortunate to have been given a platform, so we can help raise funds for teenagers with cancer.'

I was just about to leave the office when the band's PR agent rang.

'Charlotte, it's Sadie, that quote you rang me about earlier it was Dan's not Edison's.'

'Who is Dan?'

'Another band member, so you can't use it.'

'Can't use it, it's already gone down the line.'

'There's no way the band's management will allow you.'

'Our readers only recognise Edison and besides, the quote is totally innocuous.'

'Edison is really particular about his image.'

'His image, I've got teenagers here photographed bald following cancer treatment. They're not banging on about their image.'

'Edison says unless the quote is removed or re-attributed he won't speak to *The Daily News* again.'

'FFS,' I said as I slammed the phone down.

Thoughts...

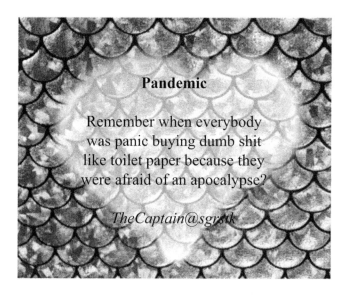

Pandemic

Remember when everybody
was panic buying dumb shit
like toilet paper because they
were afraid of an apocalypse?

TheCaptain@sgrstk

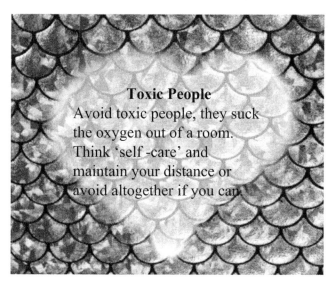

Toxic People
Avoid toxic people, they suck
the oxygen out of a room.
Think 'self-care' and
maintain your distance or
avoid altogether if you can

47: Mr. Jones

'Aktor, could I ask you a favour?' The two men were enjoying a rare coffee break in a side room, in between patients. 'How's your list looking for Thursday? Can I give you one patient?'

'Who's that, then?' said Aktor.

'Charlotte James,' said Mr. Jones

'I thought you were going to say her.'

'Why?'

'She rang in first thing this morning requesting her next appointment to be with me.'

'Oh really?' said Mr. Jones fiddling with his lanyard.

'I'm not going to ask you why you want to swap. But it sounds like she's really got under your skin.'

'I'll put her back on my list. I'll speak to her.'

'Okay,' said Aktor. 'How are things with Jasmine?'

'Really good actually, she's doing really well, back on track.'

'That's good to hear. I'd better go the coffee doesn't get any better here.' Mr. Jones smiled.

48: Charlotte

I was taken aback when I walked into the examination room, I heard Mr. Jones talking to Aktor Khan in the adjoining room. Then there was a knock at the door and Mr. Jones appeared, looking flustered. 'What's up?' he asked me.

'I thought it was the best thing to do. To ask to see Mr. Khan.'

'So, you want to see my colleague Aktor?'

'Yes, I do,' I replied.

'I'm afraid you've got me this morning, if that's okay?'

I just sat in silence, staring at Mr. Jones.

'You seem to be healing up really well,' he said as he examined me. In six months' time do you want to do nipple reconstruction and would that be under a general or local? Some patients find it very uncomfortable under a local, especially having your arms outstretched for over an hour.'

'I'm up for a local. I want to avoid having another GA.'

'Fine. And will you be requesting the lovely Aktor Khan or myself?'

'Both.'

'Both it is, Charlotte.'

Two weeks later

'Are you sure you really want to go out?' Sam asked. 'The forecast's two inches of rain later.'

'Yes, I'm sure,' I said. 'I never go out anywhere these days. I need some fresh air.'

'You don't need to go to those meetings anymore.'

'I'd like to go, my head's so full of everything.'

'Okay, if that's what you want.'

I needed to be honest with myself about Mr. Jones and Damien had been really bugging me again - calling, texting. Ever since he broke off his engagement with Stacey, he seemed to have switched his attention back to me again. He was no good without a woman to look after him.

'I'll be going out in five minutes.'

I grabbed my coat and kissed the children goodnight. Sam was right about the weather. By the time I got to the church, the meeting had already started. I was soaked; I didn't want to interrupt the meeting by going in late; I could hear lots of low murmuring already. I thought back to when Damien and I had first started going to meetings. I used to think we were the recovery couple. Damien would go to AA and I would go to Al-anon for friends and families of alcoholics. Sometimes we would walk to the same meeting venue hand-in-hand. I stopped searching for his bottles and following him to the pub, as I realized I was making it worse. Damien didn't want to stop drinking; he just wanted to please me.

I put my head under the hand drier in the toilets and flinched as it roared into life. The noise was deafening. I hoped they couldn't hear it in the meeting. The damp smell of parquet floors and wet coats in the church hallway reminded me of school. I was just about to walk through the door and take my seat when I heard a voice:

'Hello, my name's Dick and my wife's an alcoholic. She's in Halfway House.' My legs felt as though they would buckle under my own weight. Dick continued, 'This is my first meeting, and, I really don't know what I should do or not do. I don't really want to be here after all, my wife has got the problem not me. But the thing is, it's becoming a problem for me. I don't really know what to do.'

Dick looked up and caught my eye as I walked in. I scrambled to find a seat, the only empty chair was next to him. It was a tight squeeze; I felt myself fumbling around, touching his thigh by accident. I finally looked up at Mr. Jones and whispered in his ear: 'What the fuck?!'

'Charlotte. Good to see you.'

Together in a cultish unison everyone said: 'Welcome, Dick.'

He acknowledged this with a lopsided smile.

I'd never seen Mr. Jones out of his comfort zone. He was always so in control at work – at least he came across that way. It felt like a relief to know that Mr. Jones was a human being after all. I resisted the urge to hug him. The meeting flew by. The minute it was over, the chair of the meeting made a beeline for Mr. Jones as I hurried off to find my damp coat, I could see them both locked in conversation.

Coat donned I made a dash for the exit of the village hall. I usually hung around for 10 minutes afterwards for a chat, but not that day. I wanted to run. It was still raining heavily as I power-walked away from the meeting. With each step, I felt my breathing ease. As I turned a corner, lights from a nearby car beamed down on me. The electric window opened on the driver's side, and I heard my name being called: 'Get in! You look like a drowned rat!'

Window wipers going at full tilt, the car's fan heater full blast, we sat there in silence as the car steamed up.

Mr. Jones pressed a button on the car's touch screen and Nora Jones' *Come Away with Me* began to play.

'What happened in Afghanistan?' I asked.

'Now there lies a tale,' replied Dick.

49: Mr. Jones

Dick surveyed the green patchwork quilt of England disappearing as, ascending from RAF Brize Norton, they hit cloud cover. He felt a little nostalgic, seeing England from above always made him think of William Blake's *'Jerusalem'*. He and Jasmine had chosen it for the recessional song at their lavish wedding; Jasmine's boarding-school-educated father had belted out every word of it without the hymn sheet. But Dick found it hard to relax, let alone sleep, on the five-hour flight to Akrotiri, the British base in Cyprus. When he did finally doze off, he woke with a jolt as the plane began its descent.

At Akrotiri, he boarded an RAF C17 troop carrier. Mid-flight, he changed into standard issue helmet and desert camouflage body armour, a far cry from his lightweight blue hospital scrubs. The noise from the powerful military engines rendered sleep impossible, even though the red safety light gave a trance-like glow to the aircraft interior. His armour weighed him down, and any little movement caused chafing on his ill-prepared civilian skin. He felt out of place with the battle-hardened soldiers, most of them sleeping soundly, unperturbed by the flight into a warzone.

The final approach was something he had been briefed on back at Brize Norton; the near-vertical descent was a tactic to avoid ground fire. Dick was shoved forward in his seat and felt his gut tossed up inside his ribs, hampering his breathing. His jaw turned to steel until the aircraft flared out just before touchdown on the dusty plain of central Afghanistan.

He stepped out from underneath the grey metal underbelly of the aircraft. It was September, he felt the sweat breaking out on his neck – but it wasn't just the heat that made him sweat. As he observed the arid Camp Bastion, the size of Reading, he noticed layer upon layer of grit-filled cages lining the perimeter, which he guessed would be to absorb bullets from the insurgents. He thought back to his childhood, remembering the excitement of building a fortress in his back garden. But his boyish enthusiasm evaporated. He felt a tightening in his solar plexus – the reality of entering enemy territory was hitting him. As the soldiers were filing forward, he went rigid and stopped dead.

'This ain't the place for a fucking picnic, Doc,' bellowed a British voice from behind him, interrupting the autometer disembarkation as Dick stood motionless, deep in thought.

After a meal of standard military fayre in the officers' mess, he retired to the pod where he was to sleep on a fold-out bed, sharing his living space with eight other men. Too tired to think or make small talk with the soldiers around him, he just collapsed.

Hours later he woke to the sound of helicopters overhead. It seemed they were flying inches from his pod. He looked around and was comforted by the lack of movement from the soldiers. 'This is normal,' he told himself.

Following acclimatisation training, he was shown around the medical centre. At the laundry he was told to 'square his kit away', and a smiling boy called Hassan took his clothes to be washed.

'DVD sir? Only five dollars. Special price for you.'

'Not today, *shukran. Allah al hafiz.*'

Hassan broadened his grin, 'What you doing here, sir? You not like the others.'

'I'm a surgeon, here to help the wounded,' Dick replied confidently.

'Here? This camp?' Hassan asked, pointing at the makeshift medical centre that Mr. Jones had just been shown.

'No, I'm heading down to Kandahar, first thing tomorrow morning.'

'I have your kit ready then sir. Your name?'

'Richard Jones.'

****

Dick was in a convoy heading towards Kandahar. It was cramped in the back of the armoured patrol vehicle. The pungent aroma of testosterone mixed with engine oil was unfamiliar to him, a strong contrast to the disinfectant he was used to. In the distance, the burnt orange sun was rising over the mountains, obliterating his already limited view of the horizon, causing him to squint. He held his hands up to the light for inspection. His nails had grown longer and were underlaid with dirt. There'll be plenty of time to scrub them, he mused, when we get to the base.

To the right of him sat Hamid, a local doctor he had been introduced to at yesterday's training session. To the left sat Sarah, a combat medic. She was to relieve one of the soldiers on duty in Kandahar. The journey was going to be at least three hours of acute discomfort; it wasn't long before he was desperate to stretch his legs. His whole body ached. The vehicle came to a halt on the side of the barely paved road.

'Sit tight. The engineers are clearing the VP for us,' the driver announced.

'What's a VP?' Dick asked Sarah.

'A vulnerable point. Basically, anywhere that's easy to plant an IED.'

'An IED?' he queried, feeling uneasy.

'Improvised explosive device. They use them all over the place now. The guys are just checking for them, we're waiting for the all clear. Happens all the time. We'll be on our way shortly.' She smiled at him.

There was a hush as the soldiers methodically carried out their search: 20 metres forward, 20 metres to the left and 20 metres to the right.

Dick felt like a restless child. He removed his seatbelt in an attempt to stretch every part of his body in the limited space; starting with his feet, working towards his head and manoeuvring himself towards the back door which was ajar.

A pair of dark, bizarrely clown-like eyes appeared through the crack of the door. A huge flash followed by the loudest bang he had ever heard went off inside the vehicle. Dick was stunned, unable to think clearly or even to move to what he perceived as safety. He felt sharp metal at his temple: 'You doctor?'

He heard gunfire and shouting outside. He realised the metal pressed against his head was a rifle. 'What? ... Er, yes. Yes, I'm a doc ...'

The gunman dragged him out with one hand, emptying a magazine round into the vehicle with the other.

Dick was pushed backwards onto the ground. He instinctively hugged his chest, his hands hidden in his armpits. The last thing he saw was the bright blue of the sky. Then a hood was jammed over his head.

'You sit. You no move.' Dick could smell his captor's rotten teeth as he was bundled into a vehicle. The engine spluttered into life. He heard a door slam. The gunshots and shouting faded as the vehicle sped off along the dusty track.

What seemed like hours passed. It was probably only 30 minutes at the most but time stretched out with every jolt and bump of the vehicle.

With an increasing sense of panic in his chest, Dick's breathing went shallow. He knew he couldn't afford to flip out – he would blow everything he had ever worked for. He'd probably never see his family again. Survival mode, he kept telling himself. Just survive. He thought back to the times he'd been beaten up after school, and took some comfort from the fact that he had survived before but that was child's play.

The vehicle ground to a halt. He heard shouting. All of his senses were heightened. He heard the back door being wrenched open. His body froze as he prepared for yet more physical abuse.

The light splintered his eyes as his captives yanked his hood off. It took several seconds for him to come to, gasping for air. Even the hot and stale Afghan breeze gave him some relief from the hood.

He could hear what sounded like blood-curdling screams, coming from somewhere inside the compound he was in. It sounded like a woman being tortured. 'What is this place?' 'Where the fuck am I?'

He was shoved into a dimly lit makeshift tent. Inside was a heavily pregnant woman, writhing on a less than sterile improvised operating table. It was clear even before he touched her abdomen that the baby was breech, this gave very little time for a live birth.

Dick was handed a scalpel.

'You' – the man jabbed his finger into Dick's shoulder – 'Cut Inshallah.'

A small sense of relief passed over Dick; at least he knew the purpose of his capture.

He was used to working under pressure during operations in theatre, but his hands were shaking uncontrollably as he began to realise the seriousness of the situation. The man behind him shoved a rifle at his temple, the screams of the woman in front of him became full volume again.

He gestured with both palms up: 'Okay. Okay.' He had to stop himself shaking, in order to save the mother and the baby's lives as well as his own.

He had only done two C-sections before when he'd been a junior doctor. He thought of his mother to distract him from his fear. He ripped off his body armour as he approached the makeshift operating table. He could hear his mother in her calm reassuring voice: 'You can do this, son.'

Dick took a deep breath, exhaled and focused on the woman's distended belly before him. A bottle of anaesthetic was thrust into his hand. As he administered it, he leaned over, gently pressing his palm on the woman's forehead, looked straight into her dark eyes and uttered: 'You're going to be okay.'

With no disinfectant available, he began to scrub up by pouring water as hot as his hands could bear from a cast iron kettle. Once he was confident that the anaesthetic had taken effect, he made a horizontal insertion three inches below the mother's belly button. The instant he felt the scalpel cut through the wall of the abdomen, he stopped shaking. All the years of training, and his experience with his mother, came together in one god-like conduit. Whatever situation he was in, he was a surgeon first and foremost.

As he pulled the baby out, cheers went up as it drew breath and started wailing. As he cut the cord, the cheers increased, as it became clear it was a healthy boy that he had delivered. The mother just kept repeating 'Thank you, thank you. You good man, you good man.'

One of the men, who he assumed was the father, left the tent. Dick heard retching noises from outside.

He had to stop himself joining in with the cheering and congratulating. As he looked around, everyone was smiling. He smiled too as he began methodically stitching up the mother's stomach. At that point a small boy entered the tent. Dick assumed it was the baby's older brother. He looked familiar. He was carrying chains. The father of the baby re-entered the tent, and motioned towards the boy. When he had finished stitching, the boy shuffled towards him with his head down and locked the chains around his wrists and ankles. The father came across and proudly patted the boy on his back, before leading Dick away from the tent. He was marched to another section of the compound. The light was fading and with the adrenaline wearing off, Dick crouched in the corner of the dusty mud house with a small barred widow for light he now found himself in. He had assumed that he was just needed for the emergency surgery and then they would let him go. 'Why am I still here? Why the chains?'

It was yet another beautiful Afghan evening. The large sun was just setting to the west of the compound and the hysteria from the day's events were melting into a sense of calm.

A small group of men gathered around a fire, talking in murmurs - presumably Arabic. They were probably discussing what to do with their highly-trained captive, Dick thought. They had now experienced first-hand just *how* useful he could be to them; there was a lot of gesturing towards his hut.

Questions began spiralling in Dick's mind. 'How did they know where I was, where I was going and with who?' He realised there was little, to no chance of rescue. The armoured patrol vehicle had been blown up, he had no radio, no form of communication and from what he knew, there was no trace that he still existed. Feeling empty, soulless and completely drained, he closed his eyes.

50: Mr. Jones

Dick opened his eyes, thinking he was still dreaming. He began to shiver uncontrollably. It was the middle of the night, and the heat from the day's sun had long escaped into the dark cloudless Afghan sky. He half-sat half-crouched in the corner of the dusty compound. His body hurt, his ribs felt bruised, his left leg was all cut up and worst of all, his index finger on his right hand had been bent back - possibly broken. He moved towards the only light coming through slight crack in the door. As he examined his leg, he noticed dried blood had stuck his combat trousers to his various injuries. Dick immediately thought of infection, so decided to leave them alone. There was nothing he could do about it anyway.

He drifted back into his own mind, it was now that the realisations of home and family were coming through thick and fast. 'What a fool I've been, I've taken everything for granted. I just want to be back with my girls.' He thought of Izzy, Mimi and Jasmine. Jasmine was doing well in rehab, she was off the booze and we were all looking forward to being reunited as a family. My fucking ego, I've screwed it up for everyone. What was I thinking of with Charlotte? Family is my world I don't want to lose that.'

With that thought, he felt a steely determination to get through this. However, the reality was, that he was incarcerated in a compound God knows where in the middle of Afghanistan. The people that cared about him didn't know where he was. The people that did know where he was didn't care.

His train of thought was interrupted by the sound of footsteps coming towards him from outside. He instinctively moved back into the dark corner of the compound. The door slowly creaked open in the darkness and he made out a slight teenage frame - Hassan stepped into the compound carrying a bowl. Raising one finger to his lips, Hassan motioned for Dick to be quiet and handed him the bowl of what smelt like soup. Realising the betrayal, Dick grabbed it and hurled it against the wall.

Hassan looked alarmed, he put his finger to his lips again.

'Sorry, Doctor Jones. You go now,' he whispered, throwing some keys and some old clothes in Dick's direction.

And with that, Hassan was gone, leaving the solid wooden door slightly ajar.

****

'What a story. You are quite the war hero.'

'No, I'm not. I've been an idiot. I could have lost everything.'

At that moment, I leaned over and kissed Dick.

He looked surprised and said, 'We'd better get going.' In silence, he drove me back to my house.

'See you in six months.'

'Yeah, see you then. Thank you for the lift.'

'My pleasure,' he said as he sped off, not looking back.

Six months later

The day had finally come when I had finished treatment - all being well, I would be discharged. I was so relieved to stop the intravenous injections of Herceptin, given to Her-2 positive patients like myself by a district nurse. At my last home appointment, Felix was off school because he wasn't very well, I didn't have any choice but to look after him and he was at home me when the district nurse arrived.

Felix looked at me all wired up with a drip, and said: 'Mummy, are you going to die?'

'Not this week,' I said, giving him a hug, careful not to dislodge the needle in my veins.

Nipple reconstruction had been less than comfortable. I'd felt like Jesus Christ on the cross, with my arms outstretched either side of my body. I had two and a half surgeons in attendance: Mr. Jones, Aktor and Aayaan although I think he was just put there as distraction for me - because of his dazzling beauty.

Frank Sinatra played in the background and Mr. Jones had been in a playful mood; with surgical scissors gripping a sponge soaked in blood-red iodine, he'd hovered over my breasts, and had said: 'I feel like daubing this on your nose like a clown, but I guess that's not very professional.'

'It isn't really,' I replied as I felt a mild cutting sensation on my right, then my left breast.

****

It was time to take stock: the chemo, the surgery and the radiotherapy, had all taken its toll, but at least it was over and I was alive. I felt I'd made the right decision in having the other breast done as well. My octogenarian friend who had a reconstruction following breast cancer had said she'd felt a lot more confident after it, especially getting back into her bikini. 'You'll look good naked.'

That was enough for me. Breast cancer means that you have to make these decisions when you're not really right in the head, because you're so terrified and you don't know enough about it. It's akin to taking your finals at university not knowing the subject. Yet stuck in my head were Mr. Jones' wise words: 'You need to make the right decisions, so that in ten years from now you won't have any regrets.'

I felt I *had* made the right decision, having children it was a no-brainer. I couldn't risk leaving them motherless. I was also really happy with the double reconstruction. I looked normal again, so I didn't dwell on it. Sam had always said I needed a boob job, but then he's a man.

Now I was waiting for my last appointment. It was strange being back in the clinic again, it was like going back to school years later, the teachers were all different, I didn't recognise anyone. I was more nervous about seeing Mr.Jones than about the cancer itself. I didn't know how to play it.

I didn't have long to wait. Minutes later, he was in front of me. 'How are you?' he said, beaming.

'I'm okay, actually. Still standing, just about.' I guess if you wanna bounce back you will, I was tempted to say.

'Let me examine you,' he said.

I flinched as he did his examination. I'd almost forgotten, that was why I was here.

'Everything seems to be in order, you won't need any more mammograms because you don't have any breast tissue. If you're worried about anything please come and see me or BMW.'

We shook hands awkwardly. I wanted to hug him, but I did nothing. I just walked out and closed the door behind me.

I managed to get to the car park before I broke down. A part of me just disappeared and I didn't have a tissue so I used my scarf to dry my tears and wipe my nose. Unbeknown to me, I'd parked in one of the surgeons' bays – I'd wondered why there were so many prestige cars parked there. Mr. Jones had been observing me as he came out to get something from his car. He also saw me kick my tyre and fall to the ground in pain when I clocked the parking ticket stuck to my windscreen.

'Charlotte, what's up?' he said as I pulled myself up.

'What's up?' I said.

'What do you mean?'

'I don't want to say goodbye to you.'

'Charlotte, I'm married. So are you.'

'I know that. I just can't help the way I feel.'

'Look,' he was starting to get snappy and had his hands on his hips. 'I've given you great boobs. Go off and enjoy your life. You're one of the lucky ones.'

'I'm sorry. I will. Goodbye.'

'Goodbye.'

I got into the car and slammed the door shut. Tasha I really need you. I've made a total fool of myself – or should I say, a tit of myself – with the surgeon, excuse the pun. I don't know what to do. I think I've blown it with him.

I couldn't find my mobile. It was pouring with rain, I had to get out of the car to check the back seat and floor. Lashings of rain hit the fleshy gap between my top and my skinny jeans. It felt like being hit with shards of ice. I felt really cold. I started shaking. My phone was nowhere to be seen.

Ten minutes later, I was roaring down country lanes in the dark with the stereo on full blast playing, Katie Melua's *Closest Thing to Crazy*. I didn't know why I was playing it – it was my break-up song with Damien. I wasn't paying much attention to the road, my tears fell heavily like drops of blood from a deep wound, obscuring my vision. I took the bend in the road at reasonable speed, but hadn't registered I was in the middle of the road. Out of nowhere, an oncoming car accelerated towards me. Everything went into slow motion. I slammed on the brakes and the other car swerved to avoid me. There was a sound of glass and metal crunching as it hit a tree.

The driver was hunched over the steering wheel. I got out of my car, and ran over to the figure at the wheel. 'My hands, my hands.' I thought he may be concussed. 'Get something to bandage my hands.'

I ripped my scarf off from around my neck and gave it to him. It was only when he deftly looped the scarf round his hand that I recognised him.

'God I'm so sorry, I'm so sorry,' I said.

'Call an ambulance,' he barked.

'I've lost my mobile.'

'Use mine. He pointed at the glove box.'

I rang 999 and hopped into his car as we waited for the ambulance.

'Have you wiped your nose on this scarf?' he said examining it.

I apologised again.

'Very hygienic.'

'I'm supposed to be picking up my girls, which was why I left work early,' said Dick.

'I'll have to ring my wife. ... Charlotte, could you ring Jasmine and tell her there's been an accident? Tell her I'm okay, but I can't get the girls. She'll have to pick them up. I have to get to hospital and get my hands stitched.

'She's under JJ?'

'Yes, of course.'

The phone rang for ages until a male voice answered: 'Ms Jones's phone.'

'Can I speak to her?' I asked.

'Can I ask who's calling?'

'Yes. Charlotte.'

'Charlotte?'

'Damien?'

We waited in a silence, punctuated by me saying to Mr. Jones 'I'm just so sorry, I'm so sorry.'

He was under the impression that Damien was Jasmine's AA sponsor. I didn't enlighten him. Damien said Jasmine was indisposed, so she couldn't collect the children. I told Dick.

'You mean drunk,' said Dick.

I offered to collect the girls. Dick accepted.

Then I said, 'Will you be okay to go in the ambulance on your own?'

'What do you think? They all know me and will be delighted to have me as POB.'

The familiar sound of sirens could be heard in the distance.

Thoughts...

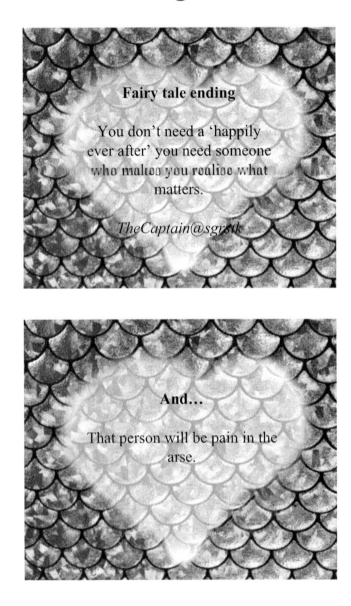

Fairy tale ending

You don't need a 'happily ever after' you need someone who makes you realise what matters.

TheCaptain@sgrstk

And...

That person will be pain in the arse.

51: Charlotte

When you're first diagnosed with cancer, five years seems a long way off. But now I was here. I had fantasised about this day. How wonderful it would be. How I would be skipping into the clinic with a big smile on my face. Screaming over an imaginary Tannoy, 'I haven't got cancer anymore!' But as with alcoholism, it's one day at a time.

I arrived at the hospital, if I'm honest, an anxious wreck. I had a leather overnight bag slung over my shoulder, as I was going to catch the afternoon flight out of Newquay to Gatwick. My father had had a stroke and as my mother was no longer with us, I was making regular trips to London to visit him. First at his home and then at his nursing home. It was difficult, especially as I was in Cornwall and he was in London.

I was scared that I wouldn't get the all clear or that this really was the last time I would ever see Mr. Jones. Worst of all, that he wouldn't be there, perhaps called away for some emergency. Part of me didn't want to see him at all. I felt overwhelmed with my life as it was. I was now a single mother. My relationship with Sam had just sort of…fizzled out. In spite of my skyward pointing implants, we had stopped having sex and fun together; this always spells the end of a relationship or so I thought. It was an amicable split; we were still great friends.

After breast cancer, you feel compelled to do something big. Conceivably, some grand gesture and make some seismic change. Such as; get married, divorced, quit your job, learn a new skill, rob a bank. Life becomes more poignant. Think of sand rushing out of the egg timer, life.

When I'd met Sam all those years ago, it had been such a relief; he was breakfast, lunch and dinner. After the chaotic years of Damien, I was happy to get some order into my life. A full fridge, and a clean house. Especially with the arrival of children. I didn't want my children brought up by an alcoholic. But I traded unmanageability for a life of quiet desperation. Meeting Mr. Jones had made me realise this. Or was it getting breast cancer? Probably both.

Both Sam and I agreed that the children came first; we would always try and act in their best interest, not winding up in court. After the incident with Natasha, things had never been the same. Sam spent more and more time at work and talked about Will incessantly. I found pictures of Will on his phone. I always thought if Sam had cheated on me it would be with a younger model. But what I hadn't seen coming was that Sam turned out to be gay and had started a relationship with Will from his work place. I was pleased for him eventually as Will was lovely and great with the kids, which eased the burden of me travelling to London every weekend.

I was, of course, nervous at the possibility of seeing Mr. Jones again. But would it be him? Would he still be there now?

I sat down in the ever so familiar waiting room. Very little had changed here, maybe a new lick of paint and some different staff faces. The sombre mood and plethora of headscarves, made it feel more like a mosque.

Five years hadn't changed the feel of this room. But I had changed.

I was single again and I quite liked it. I have spent most of my adult life in a relationship. It felt good to be free, not to have anyone commenting on what you should or shouldn't be doing. But I found evenings to be the hardest part of the day. The children would always eat early – it was the fish finger years. So, I invariably found myself eating dinner alone. I missed that sharing time, whether the day had gone well or badly, and when you have so much shared history. But I now had child-free weekends, so that I could get to London to see my dad, but I was grateful for that.

When Mr. Jones walked into the room, he saw me and his face lit up. I was, despite initial reservations, so happy to see him. I had heard snippets from Damien that Jasmine was still drinking and had separated from him. She was living in a rented flat in South Kensington near Halfway House, with Damien a regular visitor, which made sobriety impossible.

'Is it really five years?' Dick said.

'Yes,'

After methodically examining me he said: 'You're fine, medically. Go off and enjoy your life.'

I wanted to cry. He just wanted to get rid of me.

'How is that husband of yours?' he said.

'Ex-husband.'

'Ex-husband? I'm sorry to hear that.'

I wanted to just break down. Instead, I shook his hand before propelling myself out the door.

I leapt into my car with such velocity, anything to avoid another mental breakdown in the car park. It was only when the barrier went down, that I realised I'd left my bag in the examination room.

Oh Fuckery, Fuck.

Out of all the appointments, of all the clinics, in all of the hospitals, in all of the world, I leave my bloody bag in Mr. Jones' office. Deep breath...Charlotte, I thought to myself.

I went back in. Breathless, I was just about to ram the doors of the examination room when I heard Mr. Jones' voice loud and clear. I hesitated I didn't want to disturb him.

'I met with the lovely Charlotte James today,' he said into his Dictaphone. 'She's left her husband. I'm not going to wait for Jasmine to stop drinking. It was Jasmine's beauty, the idea of her, that turned my head. But I didn't really love her, I only realised this when I met Charlotte – and when you know, truly you know.'

I pushed open the door.

'Charlotte?' said Dick reddening from ear-to-ear as he swivelled round in his chair to face me.

'I thought, I'd got rid of you?'

'I forgot my bag.'

'Looks like I'm stuck with you then.'

'Well, I guess you are……………'

'I guess it's just me…and Mr. Jones.'

The End

Printed in Great Britain
by Amazon

83789657R00200